THE TWILIGHT
OF THE
NYMPHS

CLARA TICE

PIERRE LOUŸS

THE TWILIGHT
OF THE
NYMPHS

Decorations by CLARA TICE

Fredonia Books
Amsterdam, The Netherlands

The Twilight of the Nymphs

by
Pierre Louÿs

ISBN: 1-58963-962-6

Copyright © 2002 by Fredonia Books

Fredonia Books
Amsterdam, The Netherlands
http://www.fredoniabooks.com

CONTENTS

LIST OF PLATES

INTRODUCTION

READING these pastels by Pierre Louÿs, I was reminded of a remark made by a reviewer of a volume of my own prose poems, some years ago: "They induce a luxurious stupor against which the mind eventually rebels." I was never quite sure of the exact intention of this remark: but, although the two works are, alas, vastly different, it is not impossible that a similar thought might also occur to some readers of the present volume.

These charming combinations of fantasy, symbolism and mythology are far too delicate for casual reading. In the broad light of the American day, the delicate nuances of dew-tipped grasses and shadowy waters, the pale twilights over fields of asphodel, seem exotic and unreal. And, in spite of ourselves, our mind does, in a way, rebel, possibly resenting our weakness in permitting such fanciful dreams to absorb our attention or, possibly, because of our English heritage which so often makes us feel slightly ashamed at having allowed our emotions—particularly the more delicate ones—to be played upon.

It is to be regretted. We need more dreams and more dreamers. The soft voices of the nymphs would benefit and calm us infinitely more than the loud, shameless voices of the young females found between the covers of so many of our present-day books.

But we are, just now, in a state of transition: in many circles, the awakening of the national self-consciousness is well under way. We are more interested in the furniture used by our forefathers and in their direct heritage to us than we are in the more subtle heritage from that civilization which died out two thousand years ago. One of the inevitable accompaniments of such a period will be a large number of books which, in the enthusiasm of the moment, will be unduly localized. And, before this impulse will have reached its balance, no doubt, in the usual manner of reformations, it will have swept aside most of the European literary influence.

With the reaction, when it comes, the scope of our vision will again broaden, and we will turn once more to the best of the foreign authors: but with more discretion, then, and without the blind idolization of past decades, to supplement, but never again to dominate, our own literature and thought.

In that future day, Pierre Louÿs should be remembered. Aside from his other works, these pastels, intangibly beautiful, pale and shadowy as the realm described by Dionysos, have too enduring an appeal to be ignored, even by the unknown Americans of posterity. And the gods and the nymphs, although they may have passed from the earth, are immortal in literature.

Pierre Louÿs retells these legends so beautifully that, under the spell of his relation, one almost loses sight of the extent to which their consummate literary craftsmanship reveals the master of literary technic no less than the imaginative artist. The pastels are not so sensational as some of the Author's other works but, in a general sense, they are the most delicate and the most sympathetic of all his writings.

As for the actual fables, those of Leda, who was visited by Zeus under the form of a swan, and of Danae, for whom the same lover appeared as a shower of gold, are well known, together with the other amorous adventures of the Father of the Gods, whose passion for virginity seemed in no way appeased by Hera's special arrangements to renew her own once each year. The fable of Danae, and that of Ariadne, as usually related, do not end quite so disastrously for the heroines.

Byblis is one of the lesser known myths, her affection for her brother, which Pierre Louÿs certainly handles with great delicacy, apparently being considered unsuitable for the ordinary, popular Mythology.

"The House upon the Nile," the one story without a mythological foundation, is really a variation on the theme of the Author's famous romance, "Aphrodite."

With the exception of "Danae," which was not published in book form until it appeared in the Collected Edition, these stories appeared at intervals between 1893 and 1898, each as a small, separate book. These little paper-covered booklets are now very scarce and, partly on this account, the Collected Edition was published, only a few months before the Author's death.

From this Collected Edition, the present translation has been made. The text presents some slight variations from that of the original editions but, in all such cases, has been followed as doubtless representing the matured thought of the Author. According to a note in the French edition, he had purposed, but *apparently never written, two additional pastels, with the idea of forming a collection to be called "The Heptameron of Amaryllis."*

The collection as it stands, ends with the story of Danae, without any conclusion or the reappearance of Amaryllis and her companions, the Author's work ending with the words "any longer here." In order to cover the natural comment on Danae's adventure, and to soften the ending of the collection as a whole, I have ventured to add a short conclusion, a considerable liberty, but one which I trust may be forgiven, particularly as the intention in the ending of Amaryllis' relation is somewhat obscure.

M. S. BUCK.

Philadelphia.
New Year's Day 1927.

THE TWILIGHT
OF THE
NYMPHS

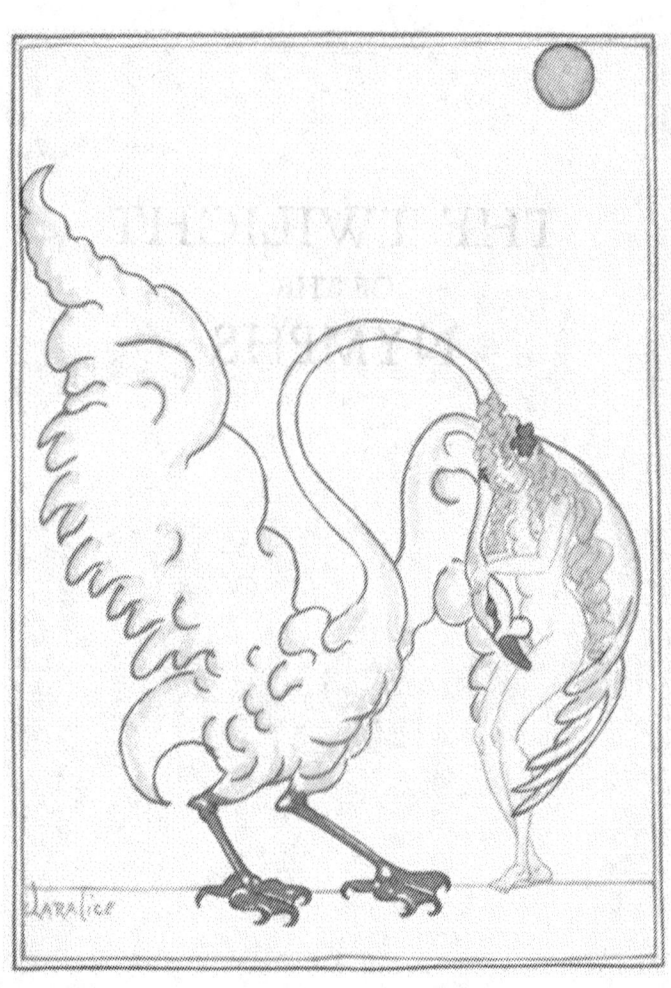

LEDA

or

The Glory of Blessed Darkness

ONE could no longer see. An invisible Artemis hunted beneath the crescent moon inclined beyond the black branches which swarmed with stars. The four Corinthians remained lying upon the grass near the three young men; and one scarcely knew whether any would venture to speak again, so silent was the hour.

Stories should be told only in bright daylight. When the shadows have entered, one can no longer hear fabulous voices, for the wandering spirit settles itself and communes enchantingly with itself.

Each of the outstretched women already had a secret companion which she created charmingly to the real image of her childish desire. However, they all opened their eyes in the darkness when solemn Melandryon spoke these first words:

"I will relate to you the history of the Swan and of the little nymph who lived upon the banks of the river Eurotas. It is to the glory of blessed darkness."

He half raised himself, resting one hand among the grasses, and began to speak thus:

I

IN those times, there were no tombs beside the roads nor temples upon the hills.

Few men existed; no one spoke. The earth abandoned itself to the pleasure of the gods and assisted the birth of monstrous divinities. Those were the times in which Echidna gave birth to the Chimera and Pasiphæ to the Minotaur. Little children paled in the woods, frightened by the flight of dragons.

Upon the humid borders of the river Eurotas, where the woods were so dense that one never saw the sunlight, there lived an extraordinary young girl who was bluish like the night, mysterious as the slender moon and soft as the milky-way. Because of this, she was called Leda.

She was really almost blue for, in her veins, ran the blood of the iris and not, as in yours, the blood of roses. Her nails were bluer than her hands, her nipples bluer than her breasts; her elbows and her knees were wholly azure. Her lips shone with the color of her eyes which were blue as the deep water. As for her flow-ing hair, it was sombre and blue as the nocturnal sky and quickened so along her arms that she seemed to have wings.

She loved only the water and the night. Her pleasure was in walking over the spongy fields along the shores, where one feels the water without seeing it, and her naked feet shivered with pleasure at the hidden moisture.

For she never bathed herself in the river, fearing the jealous naiads; and, beside, she did not wish to give herself completely to the water. But how she loved to get wet! She would dip the extreme ringlet of her hair in the rapid current and then trail it in slow circling designs over her pale skin. Or she would take a little of the fresh water in the hollow of her hand and let it run between her young breasts and lose itself in the fold of her rounded legs. Or else she would lie extended on the damp moss and drink softly from the surface of the water, like a silent hind.

This was her life; and the thought of the satyrs. These were sometimes seen by accident, but they always fled away in fright, for they took her for Phoebe who was severe to those who saw her naked. She would have liked to talk with them if they would have paused near her. The details of their appearance filled her with amazement. One night, when she had gone a little way into the forest, because rain had fallen and the earth was flooded, she had seen closely one of these demi-gods, asleep; but she, in her turn, had taken fright and had withdrawn quickly. Afterward, she would pass there at intervals, uneasy over things which she did not understand.

She began to regard herself also, and found herself mysterious. This was a period when she became very sentimental and wept in her hair.

When the nights were clear, she looked at herself in the water. At one time she thought it might be better to gather and roll up her hair in order to bare her neck which, she perceived, was pretty under her caressing hand. She chose a supple rush to hold the blue knot of her hair, and made herself a drooping coronal with five large aquatic leaves and a languishing water lily.

At first she took pleasure in walking about thus. But no one saw her, for she was alone. Then she became unhappy and ceased playing with herself.

Now, her spirit did not know it, but already her body awaited the beating of the Swan's wings.

II

ONE evening, when she was scarcely awake and reflecting on resuming her dreams, because a long stream of yellow day still gleamed beyond the night of the forest, her attention was drawn by a noise in the near-by reeds, and she saw a Swan appear.

The beautiful bird was white as a woman, splendid and roseate as the day, and radiant as a cloud. He seemed the very spirit of the noon-day sky, its form, its winged essence. That is why he was called Zeus.

Leda watched him as he moved with spread wings. At a distance, he circled about the nymph, gazing sideways at her. After that, he drew closer and, raising himself on his wide, red feet, stretched the undulous grace of his neck as high as he could, over the bluish young thighs, to the soft fold of the hip.

Leda's astonished hands gently touched the little head, enveloping it with caresses. The bird quivered in all his feathers. In his deep, soft wings, he clasped and bent her naked legs. Leda let herself fall upon the ground.

She put her two hands over her eyes. She felt, not fear, nor shame, but an inexplicable joy; and her beating heart lifted her breasts.

She divined nothing of what was going

to happen. She did not know what could happen. She understood nothing, not even why she was happy. She felt, along her arms, the supple neck of the Swan.

Why had he come? What had she done, that he should come? Why had he not flown away like the other swans on the river or the satyrs of the forest? From her earliest memories, she had always lived alone. Therefore she had not many ideas for thought and the happenings of this night were so disconcerting . . . This Swan . . . this Swan . . . She had not called him, she had not even seen him, for she was asleep. And he had come.

She was no longer afraid to look at him, and did not move for fear of making him fly away. She felt, upon her hot cheeks, the freshness of his beating wings.

29

Soon he seemed to recoil and his caresses changed. Leda opened herself to him like a blue flower of the river. She felt between her cold knees the warmth of the bird's body. Suddenly she cried:

"Ah! . . . Ah! . . ."

And her arms q u i v e r e d like pale branches. The beak had penetrated her, frightfully, and, within her, the head of the Swan moved violently, as though he were deliciously devouring her entrails.

Then she gave a long sob of abundant felicity. With closed eyes, she let her burning head fall backward, tore with her fingers at the grass and shivered in the air her little, convulsed feet which finally spread themselves out in the silence.

For a long time, she remained motion-less. At the first movement she made, her hand met, upon her, the ensanguined beak of the Swan.

She sat up and saw the great white bird against the clear sheen of the river.

She wished to arise; the bird obstructed her.

She wished to take a little water in the hollow of her hand and cool her joyous pain; the bird stopped her with his wing.

Then she took him in her arms and cov' ered with kisses his tufted plumes which bristled up under her mouth. Afterwards, she stretched out on the bank and slept heavily.

The next morning, at the break of day, a new sensation awoke her suddenly, and it seemed to her that something detached itself from her body. And this was a large, blue egg which had rolled in front of her, gleaming like a sapphire.

She wished to take it and play with it or perhaps to bake it in hot embers as she had seen the Satyrs do, but the Swan seized it in his beak and placed it under a cluster of bending reeds. He stretched his wings over it, regarding Leda fixedly, and then, in a straight flight toward the sky, slowly mounted so high that he disappeared in the brightening dawn with the last pale star.

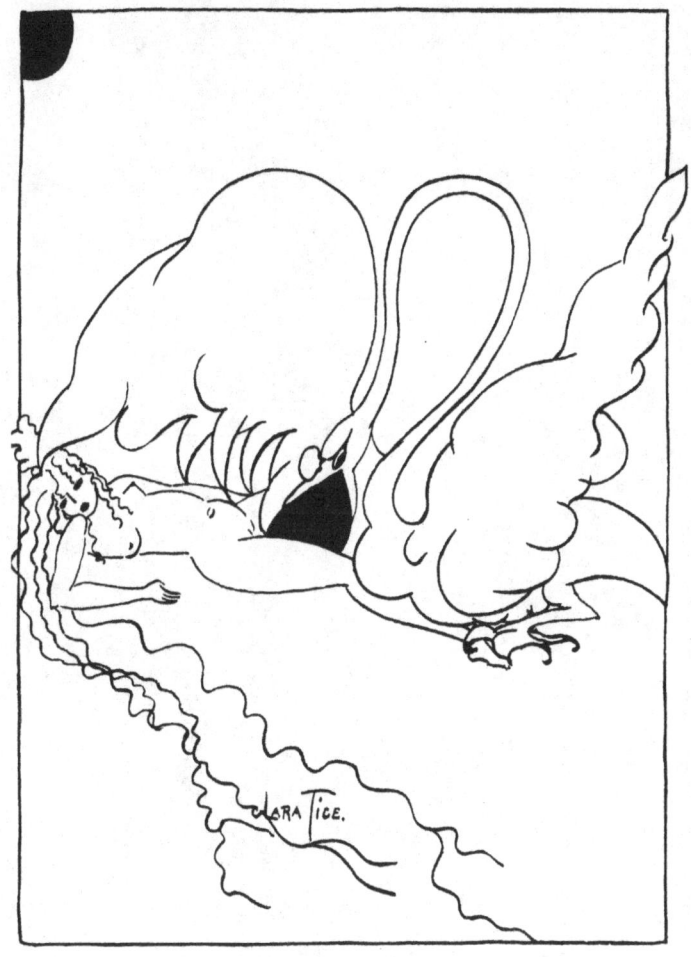

III

LEDA hoped that, at the next rising of the stars, the Swan would return to her, and she awaited him among the reeds of the river, near the blue egg which had been born of their miraculous union.

The Eurotas was peopled with swans, but this one was no longer there. She would have recognized him among a thousand and, even with her eyes closed, she would have sensed his approach. But he was no longer there; of this she was quite sure.

Then she removed her coronal of water

leaves, let it fall in the stream, shook down her blue hair and wept into it.

When she wiped her eyes and looked about, a satyr, whose steps she had not heard, stood there.

For she was no longer like Phoebe. She had lost her virginity. The satyrs were no longer afraid of her.

She bounded to her feet and drew back in fright. The ægipan said to her, gently:

"Who art thou?"

"I am Leda," she replied.

He was silent for a moment, then resumed:

"Why art thou not like the other nymphs? Why art thou blue like the water and the night?"

"I do not know."

He regarded her in great astonishment.

"What dost thou here, all alone?"

"I await the Swan."

And she looked towards the river.

"What swan?" he asked.

"The Swan. I did not call him, I had never seen him, and he came. I am so astonished. I will tell thee."

She related to him what had happened, and she parted the reeds to show him the blue egg of the morning.

The satyr understood. He began to laugh and gave her coarse explanations which she stopped at each word by putting her hand over his mouth; and she exclaimed:

"I do not wish to know. I will not. Oh! Oh! thou hast told me — Oh! is this possible! Now I can no longer love him and I shall be unhappy enough to die."

He seized her by the arms, passionately.

"Do not touch me!" she wept. "Oh! how happy I was this morning! I did not know how happy I was! Now, if he re-returns, I shall no longer love him. Now thou hast told me! Ah, how wicked thou art!"

He clasped her suddenly and caressed her hair.

"Oh! No! No! No! . . . No!" She cried again. "Oh! not thee! Oh! not that! Oh! the Swan! If he should return . . . Alas! Alas! All is ended, all is ended."

She remained with open eyes, without weeping, her mouth open, her hands trembling with fright.

"I wish I could die. I know not even whether I am mortal. I wish I could die in the water, but I am afraid of the naiads and that they would carry me away with them. Oh! What have I done!"

And she sobbed loudly upon her arms.

But a grave voice spoke before her and, as she opened her eyes, she saw the god of the river, crowned with green grasses, who stood half out of the water, leaning upon an oar of bright wood.

He said:

"Thou art the night. And thou hast loved the symbol of all which is bright and glorious, and thou hast united thyself to it.

"From the symbol is born the symbol and from the symbol shall be born Beauty. It is in the blue egg which has come forth from thee. Since the beginning of the

world, it was known that she would be
called Helen; and he who shall be the last
man shall know that she lived.

"Thou has been filled with love because thou hast known nothing. That is
the glory of blessed darkness.

"But thou art also a woman and, on the
evening of the same day, man also has im-
pregnated thee.

"Thou bearest within t h y s e l f the
shadowy being who knows nothing of itself; whom its father has not foreseen and
whom its son would ignore. I shall take
the germ in my waters. It shall remain in
nothingness.

"Thou hast been full of hatred because
thou hast learned all. And I will make
thee forget all. This is the glory of blessed
darkness."

She did not quite understand what he had said, but she thanked him, weeping.

She entered into the bed of the river and purified herself there of the satyr. And, when she returned to the bank, she had lost all remembrance of her sorrow and of her joy.

*
* *

Melandryon ceased speaking. The women remained silent. However, Rhea finally asked:

"And Castor and Polydeuces? Thou hast said nothing of them. They were Helen's brothers."

"No. That is a wrong legend, they were not concerned. Helen, only, sprang from the Swan."

39

"How knowest thou?"

"..."

"And why sayest thou that the Swan wounded her with his beak? That is not in the legend and it is not probable . . . And why sayest thou that Leda was blue like water at night? Thou hast a reason for saying that."

"Didst thou not hear the words of the River? Symbols should never be explained. They should never be penetrated. Have belief. Ah! Do not doubt. That which figures as a symbol hides a truth, but it is not made manifest for, otherwise, why should it be symbolized.

"Forms should not be rent, for they conceal only the Invisible. We know that there are adorable nymphs enclosed in the trees and that, when the woodcutter opens

40

them, the hamadryads are already dead. We know that, behind us, there are dancing satyrs and divine nudities; but we should not turn: all would have already disappeared.

"The undulous reflection of the springs is the essence of the naiad. The buck standing amidst the goats is the essence of the satyr. One or another among you is the essence of Aphrodite. But it is not to be spoken, it is not to be known, one should not try to understand it. Such is the condition of love and of happiness. That is the glory of blessed darkness."

ARIADNE

or

The Road of Eternal Peace

*N*OW, *having come to a cavern, the most profound, the most sombre of all the forest, so deserted by beasts and men that the very silence seemed to have smothered itself and given place to something still more inexpressible, the Corinthians recoiled a little, raising their hands to their temples, opened their eyes without seeing and, without speaking, opened their lips.*

Trembling, for they felt themselves allured by the darkness, they pressed close to one another, as the poor little souls of the dead press together before the portal of Hades in an effort to remain without.

The voice of Thrases drew them from their benumbed terror.

"Assuredly," he said, "this is one of the entrances to Tartarus; but there is no need to be frightened; none of you will see the black torches of Persephone before the day fixed by the Keres. Moreover, that is a happy day which should be welcomed with joy . . ."

"I do not wish to die," said Rhea.

"O Thrases, what art thou saying?" asked wise Amaryllis. "For death troubles me also, and my soul cannot remain indifferent when I dream of the tomb."

But Thrases did not argue, in order to avoid the weariness of too obvious reflections, and, for his own pleasure, involved his thought in an obscure and subtle story.

The Corinthians had seated themselves on a long block of polished rock. He, meanwhile, remained standing near Clinias and Melandryon, the first too distracted to understand, the second too wise to listen.

He began slowly, as though he feared to speak, and his phrases were short, his voice hesitating and feeble.

I

A FOREST of cedars.

Evening.

Seven young men and seven young girls advanced, holding each other by the hand.

They had come from Attica, upon a ship with black sails.

And one of them was Theseus, son of Aegeus, son of Pandion, son of Cecrops, son of Erechtheus.

Green palms! coronals of oak leaves! cries! triumphs! laurels! outstretched hands! accompany the Heroes . . .

Accompany the Heroes . . .

They had come from Attica, upon a ship with black sails.

And all, during the funereal journey, had pledged themselves, two by two, to find each other again, beyond death, among the indolent fields of asphodel.

Beyond the horrible death for which they were destined by the human Bull, fruit of the shame of Pasiphæ.

They had pledged themselves. Yet two among them remained apart: the hero Theseus, confident in his hands, and the virgin Myris who walked near him.

And evening ascended over the earth.

Under the horizontal foliage of the cedars, through the thin plantings of the forest, the long rays from the west ran out like the blades of swords, impalpable and transparent.

50

The condemned ones, two by two, slowly traversed these great weapons of the sun. They knew exactly how many they would meet before reaching the entrance of the Labyrinth. And after the last would come the terrible night.

At least, this they believed, but Theseus, and Myris like him, had other certainties.

They advanced.

They advanced.

At last they arrived.

But they had not yet passed the last ray of the sun when they heard, behind them, a quick step on the dead leaves.

They turned: there stood a woman.

She was of large stature, well shod with tight leather straps and clad in the short tunic of the followers of Artemis. The white cloth, fastened at the shoulders with two clasps of beaten gold, was drawn in at the girdle, leaving her dainty knees uncovered. A silver diadem gleamed beneath the rich ornament of her hair, of which part was disposed in plaits and part tucked up in a Laconian knot, with more grace than artifice. And in her eyes, so brown and yet so clear, such high spirit shone that she seemed to all to be the princess of Crete, Ariadne, daughter of Minos and grand-daughter of the Sun.

She made a sign: Theseus approached. She made another sign: the others turned and drew back a little to an opening which still flamed with the lingering red of the west.

She, still panting and with hot cheeks, smiled, half closing her eyes. She extended her arms and drew aside the heavy, dark curls on the Hero's temples . . .

"Thou art handsome," she said, happily.

He remained silent. She ignored this, and continued:

"Ah! I know well that thou goest to slay the Minotaur and that all the Gods will lend their weight to thine arm when thou shatterest that wild, surly muzzle upon the stones. But how wilt thou come out from that inextricable crypt? Triumphant, and holding upraised the disgusting head of the Recluse, thou wouldst die in the enclosed passages, between two walls always the same; and that which Strength should have accomplished, dull Forgetfulness would allow to perish. Thou knowest not that this palace is a labyrinth of stone and that those who enter it cannot release themselves. But I have thought of thee, son of Pandionian Aegeus, and, in the space between my breasts, I have brought thee safety."

She slipped her hand into her tunic and drew out a green ball.

"See," she said. "This is my Miletian thread. It is fine like one of my hairs and as long as the circuit of the island. With it I could weave green shifts for all the nymphs of this forest or a floating veil for the sea. Take it. Thou wilt unwind it all before reaching the distant dwelling of the Monster. And thou wilt follow it in returning to the day."

She turned toward the victims.

"Go," she cried. "You are saved."

They fled. Myris did not move.

Theseus accepted the ball of thread and asked:

"Who art thou?"

"I am thine."

"Can I not name thee?"

"Ariadne, sevenfold daughter of Zeus by the grand-parents of my father who is Minos, King of Crete. But if some other name pleases thee, say it and it shall be mine."

As though he were establishing a land-mark, he gazed into Ariadne's eyes. Then, without speaking again, he entered the Labyrinth.

"Theseus! Theseus!" she called.

"Theseus, stop! I cannot wait; I want to go! I want to see thee! Oh! I am eager to assist in thy bloody victory. Together!

55

It is I who will carry the thread, and when thou hast overthrown the Beast I will kiss thy fair hands bruised by his horns, and thou shalt be my husband upon the field of thy triumph."

When she followed his steps into the Dedalian night, she fastened the pendant end of the green thread to a rock; but when she emerged, in the arms of the Hero, letting the thread run through her closed hand, the anchor which connected them with life was the poor body of Myris, strangled.

II

BETWEEN the forests and the sea.

The morning.

A little beach, rounded, pure and yellow.

Ariadne, sleeping on the Isle of Naxos, awakened without opening her eyes, for she wished to recall in her spirit all that had happened since that first day when the sight of Theseus had brought to birth within herself a second, unknown Ariadne.

The cedars — the blades of sunlight — the opening of the abysmal edifice — the victims clad in white—the Hero without weapons or helmet — the thread — the anchor—the pathway—the sharply-turning circuits — the interminable descent — the interminable ascent—the Beast—the slavering nostrils — the horns — the monstrously great hands — the short struggle — the blood upon the earth — the return through the shadows — the adorable return of day— the dew upon the tips of the grasses—the evening upon the tops of the cedars—the leisurely journey—the departure—the first movement of the vessel — the fragrance of the sea — the color of the night— the freshness of the dawn — and the second day—and the second twilight—and the landing.

She knew that she had slept close to the Slayer, side by side with his glory, and she awakened in perfect felicity before the horizon of a life equally happy and certain.

Her hand stretched out. Her hand fell upon the earth. Her hand searched, turned, and drew back, astonished. Everywhere grass or sand or cold flowers or mud.

She called:

"Theseus!"

She opened her eyes and her mouth, raised herself, lifted her two arms; and a frightened sweat crept through her hair. Neither beside her, nor before her, nor at her feet, nor in her arms . . .

She ran toward the sea. The vessel had left its moorings.

Far away, half upon the sky and half upon the water, a little black bird was flying, the rapid ship which bore the fortune of Theseus, so far away that the eye could scarcely see it and a despairing cry would die before reaching it.

Folly! She entered the sea, throwing her tunic upon the pebbles. The waves slapped against her shuddering thighs. The water mounted to her belly.

She cried:

"O Poseidon, King of the Glaucous Fields, Guardian of the Waters! Lift me up! bear me to him; he is my very self . . ."

Poseidon heard, but granted nothing. A miraculous water ravished the pleading Ariadne and threw her gently upon the thick moss.

And the vessel had disappeared forever beyond the wall of the sea.

At that instant, an uproar, a multitude,

60

cries of adulation, crackling steps on the soil of the forests.

"Io! Evoë! Who is upon the road? Who is upon the road?"

Down the mountain came Bacchantes and Satyrs and Pans, the procession hurried along by the thyrses.

"Who is upon the road? Who is in the dwelling? Iacchos! Iacchos! Evoë!"

Their hands waved branches of trees and shook garlands of ivy. Their hair was so laden with flowers that their necks bent backward; the folds of their breasts were rivulets of sweat, their thighs glowed like setting suns and their shrieks were spotted with flying foam.

"Iacchos! Beautiful God! Mighty God! Living God! Iacchos! Leader of the Orgy! Iacchos! Impulse and Guide! Incite the multitude! Drive the rout and the rapid feet! We are thine! We are thy swelling breath! We are thy turbulent desires!"

Then: suddenly they saw Ariadne.

They precipitated themselves, grasped her arms and her legs, they twisted her disordered hair; the first seized her head and, bracing a foot on her shoulder, wrenched it off, like a heavy flower; others scattered the members; the sixth tore open the belly and pulled out the little womb; and the seventh, digging into the chest, uprooted the vomiting heart.

The God, the God appeared!

They hurled themselves toward him, brandishing their trophies.

He was nude, crowned with vine leaves. A fawn skin hung upon his loins.

He carried a rod of box-wood. He said:

"Leave these poor members."

The Bacchantes threw them upon the ground and, impelled by a gesture, rushed off up the mountain, like a flock stung by bees.

Then he inclined his hollow rod which gushed out marvelously; and the members reunited, the heart awoke suddenly, and deluded Ariadne raised herself upon one hand.

"O Dionysos!" she said.

Night, clear and sombre lay over the sea.

The God stretched out his fingers and said, in a grave, tender voice:

"Arise! I am Awakening.

63

"Arise! I am Life.
"Give me thy hand . . .
"Come with me . . .
"This is the Road of Eternal Peace . . ."

III

A HIGH, bare ravine.

Night.

Peace.

"What happened?" asked Ariadne. "I no longer know his name and yet I recall that he abandoned me."

"It happened," responded the God, "it happened that he left thee, for that is the law of the love in which thou didst rely. Those who demand shall not be loved; those who shall be loved shall go. And this is why thou didst deceive thyself. But today thou art upon the true road, upon the Road of Eternal Peace."

"O King Dionysos, what then is this peace?"

"Thou feelest it not?"

"It is true. I am no longer Ariadne. I no longer feel the stones nor the leaves which, in former times, bruised my feet. I no longer feel even the freshness of the air. I feel thy hand."

"Still, I am not touching thee."

"Where dost thou lead me, Adored God?"

"To where thou shalt never again see the sun too glittering nor the night too shadowy. To where thou shalt never again feel hunger nor thirst nor love nor fatigue. From the worst of evils, the fear of death, Ariadne, thou are delivered for, in truth, thou art already dead. And, see, what happiness!"

"Oh! Could I but believe that one can be happy without pernicious Love."

"Look at me . . ."

"I see thee without it. I see thee. O Saviour! Where dost thou conduct me?"

"The land which thou goest to frequent is indeterminate, crepuscular, unchanging, colorless, airy. The grasses there are like the flowers, pale as the sky and the water. The air is always still; and the light is mysterious like a winter's day or a night of summer. One knows not whether day mounts over the earth or descends into the lower firmament. The buds never close, the petals no longer fall, there are no birds among the branches, and the up-roar of six thousand million souls is an

67

inexpressible silence. Thou shalt no longer have eyes: what wouldst thou see? Thou shalt no longer have hands: of what use to touch? Thou shalt no longer have lips: thou shalt be delivered from the kiss. But the shadow of reality shall subsist about thee, the survival of a dream without joy and without regret; without desire and without pleasure, thou shalt no longer know sorrow."

"Dost thou also inhabit this land which thou dost promise me at last?"

"I am the Ruler of the Shades, the Master of the Infernal Water. I sit upon a throne of shadows; my upraised finger draws the souls to it and, from the farthest ends of the earth, they come, whirling, yielding, beating their wings beneath my glance. I bear a coronal of vine leaves for, even as the cut grapes revive under the feet in the press and stream forth in scarlet wine, so the anguish of death is miraculously transfigured in the intoxication of resurrection. And I carry in my hand a blade of ripe wheat for, as the corrupt grain is born again in the nurturing earth and sprouts forth in living herbage, so pain and trouble germinate, flower, become ecstatic, in the great eternal peace whither thou goest."

"Shall I be far from thee, a poor soul alone in the multitude?"

"No: thou shalt reign, thou also, at my side, O Queen with beautiful hair! And thou shalt reflect, on thy face, the ineffable calm of the subterranean fields. It is thou the dead souls shall see first, and thou shalt have this joy which is refused even

69

to the Gods: that of seeing the birth of felicity in the forever-calm eyes of incorruptible Spirits."

"O Dionysos! . . ."

And she raised her arms toward him.

*

* *

"Is that all?" asked Philinna.

"I shall say no more."

And Rhea, disconcerted:

"But it is Persephone who is queen of the underworld!"

"Yes," said Thrases.

Then Melandryon, who had listened to the end of the mythological story, drew aside the narrator and, regarding him with a penetrating eye:

70

"Thou hast not told all that was in thy mind."

"No. When Dionysos had spoken thus to the daughter of Minos, the truth is that he annihilated her. But, by the simple description of so happy a future, had he not given her more joy than he promised her in it? I proceeded to do for these women what he did for Ariadne. Do not open their eyes. It is better to give confidence than to fulfill oaths, for hope is sweeter than conquest."

"Regret is sweeter than hope."

"Women do not know that."

THE HOUSE UPON THE NILE

or

The Semblance of Virtue

$\mathcal{A}$MARYLLIS stretched out languidly upon the moss and, with the tip of her willow branch, touched the hand of the youngest man.

"Speak in thy turn, Clinias," she said. "I would like a story from thee."

Clinias hesitated for some time.

"I still remember the legends which everyone knows; but I know not how, like Thrases, to mould them according to my humor, nor how, like thee, Amaryllis, to enliven them by the charm of words. I will tell what my friend Bion of Clazomenae told me, on his return from Ethiopia."

"Is it a true story?" asked Rhea.

"Yes. But I would like to have you take it for a fable and to have the personages seem to be followed by the shadow of their symbol. If I had any talent, it would not be much trouble for me to make this short history a poem in hexameters. Perhaps simply to generalize it."

The sun glared hotly above the tall forest, and the coolness under the leaves was the more delicious. Spots of light caressed Lampito who had drawn her hair over her face to protect her closed eyes. Amaryllis remained near Rhea. Philinna played with her hands. Melandryon gazed at the ground.

Then Clinias began thus:

I

ABOVE Thebes and Hermonthis, above Silsila and Ombos, Bion had ascended the Nile. He had even passed the Elephantine Isle where the territory of Egypt ends, and had advanced toward black Ethiopia which is close to the edge of the world.

He had no boat with which to over- come the slow course of the river, for he would have needed slaves to handle the oars and he was apprehensive of depend- ing on disinterested companions. Therefore he journeyed on foot along the damp, grassy banks so narrow that the path sometimes ran along the foot of multi-colored cliffs from which stretched back the monotonous infinity of the Desert.

This narrow band of living earth between two dull solitudes, this road of golden fields and of splendid herbage, split to the two horizons by the luminous green of the Nile, resounded to the cries of birds, strident and thronging, in the air, upon the water, under the tall grasses, swarming among the bare branches of the fat baobabs like perpetual, deafening locusts.

Ostriches and giraffes ran over the distant wastes; herds of antelopes fled like yellow clouds; monkeys hung suspended in fantastic groups from the supple branches of the sycamores, and occasion-

78

ally, in the mud of the Nile, where the slender steps of the ibises followed each other like long flowers, Bion contemplated with astonishment the formidable human imprint left by that mysterious Amanit, the beast upon which no man dared look but of which the Ethiopians told strange stories. And Bion, uneasy, was persuaded that the Colossi of rose granite, sculptured in the mass of the mountains, came in the solitary nights to bathe themselves to the knees in the holy river which is the father of all.

For, so far from Thebes and Memphis, the remains of Egyptian splendor still endured in an impious land. Long since, the Autochthons had retaken the land from the conquerors and yet the face of Rhameses was forever engraved upon the cliffs, for the rulers of the North had given their form to the rocks which the chisel of slaves had subdued but which neither time nor Zeus had destroyed.

It was winter. The nights were filled with cool mist. The ethereal days were still oppressive. Bion sought the shade and the springs in the forests of mimosas where lions withdrew from the sun to issue only at the rising of the night. There also lived the men, barricaded in their cabins behind palisades of date palms. Bion was their guest, night after night, leaving them in the early morning.

II

THEN, one evening . . .

"At last!" cried Lampito.

"Thou speakest well," said Philinna, politely, "but thou art too pompous. Then too, why hast thou given us a little description of Egypt before beginning thy story? I suppose that has nothing to do with the course of the adventure?"

"Be indulgent," responded Clinias. "The story of Bion is very simple, I could relate it to you in a very few words, but, after that, another would have to be found, and the heat will not permit that effort of my imagination. For the other part, it is a short scene which should not be expanded. It was necessary that I prepare with some unnecessary phrases, if I wished to give a story of the same length as the others. All this is unanswerable. Do not interrupt me again."

" . . . One evening, as he had walked a long time under a painful radiance and his weary feet were marked by their narrow straps, he approached a brown and green house raised alone on the bank of the Nile with dry mud and interwoven grasses. The heavy heads of many palms bent about it and it was so overrun by large flowering water grasses that one might say it was floating upon the same water or in jeopardy in a marsh.

Motionless, his shoulder resting against a tree, Bion regarded it.

Two young girls, before the door opening, talked together, sometimes laughing.

The elder was clad in a full, blue, fringed garment, gathered under the arms and falling to her knees. Her abundant, dark hair was separated in a thousand thin strands which closely framed a face with shining eyes and thick lips and fell only as far as the delicate, full shoulders. She bent her loins over a low bar. She laughed a little and tossed her head.

The younger was not dressed, for she was still a child. She held herself seated upon her heels, her head bent between her knees, and stuck little yellow flowers between her outspread toes.

He regarded them with interest, without coming nearer. He contemplated the House. This spot, mysterious, like anything which appears for the first time, seemed protected by its air of strangeness, solitude and uncertainty. A family lived there. For how long a time? What kind of sadness and of furtive happiness had made this hut of mud and branches joyous or gloomy? Who had built it? Who had inhabited it? What deaths, what births, had it sheltered? He felt that all this which he could imagine told him nothing about it and that this lost corner would remain always impenetrable to him.

Evening ascended rapidly. At last Bion came up.

Immediately the two girls, with little cries, drew back toward the open house. But he did not approach, and said, simply:

"I ask for hospitality."

"Father is in the fields," responded the elder. "Wait until he comes. He will receive thee."

Bion rested his arm against a tree and turned his eyes toward the Nile, annoyed by the curious regards which fixed themselves on his person.

Long after sunset, the Ethiopian arrived, following a yellow ox with tapering horns. And when he appeared, the two girls both began speaking at once.

"There is a stranger. — He asks for hospitality. — Yes, he is alone. — There, by the tree. — We would not let him enter until thy return. — Have we done right, father?"

The master took three steps in the darkness and said in a high voice:

"Be welcome. Enter my house."

When they had entered the room, and it had been lightened by lamps of baked earth:

"Here is water, bread and fruits," said the Ethiopian.

They drank and ate. And the host remained silent, feeling it would be indiscreet to ask questions for which the answers had not already been offered.

She whose brown body was draped with blue brought in the food and poured water from the jars. The younger sister had drawn back against the earthen wall, and, her hands pressed over her mouth, was considering the Stranger.

When the meal was finished, the host arose.

"It is time to go to thy bed. I know the

duties of hospitality. Here are my two daughters. The youngest has not yet known a man but she is of an age to come to thee. Go, and take thy pleasure with her."

Bion was not unfamiliar with this custom and he venerated it as a tradition of singular virtue. The gods often visited the earth, dressed as travelers, soldiers or shepherds, and who could distinguish a mortal from an Olympian who did not wish to reveal himself? Bion was, perhaps, Hermes? He knew that a refusal on his part would be taken as an insult; thus he was neither surprised nor troubled when the elder girl bent toward him and uncovered her young breasts so that he might kiss them.

Without speaking, without moving,

the child watched their offence and poised herself, her head forward, her hands relaxed as though in a dream.

After an instant of paleness, trembling, close to tears, she precipitated herself through the open door. The night closed about her.

Then the father, raising his eyes, also walked to the threshold and peered into the heavy darkness where his daughter had carried away forever the lost honor of his house.

III

THE sun was shining when Bion awakened and took up his skin bag to continue his way. The house was deserted.

He regretted not encountering the Host, but was not astonished at not seeing his companion of the night. She was too wise to expose herself to a farewell.

He began his walk.

The road which he followed beside the reeds of the Nile was so dazzling that he soon abandoned it for a little path which crossed the marshy fields towards the woods.

A sluggish hippopotamus had crushed a whole field of rice beneath his vast, purplish flesh, and lay surrounded by the devastation he had caused. Bion passed him quickly. A little while after, he entered the shadow of the mimosas.

A joyous cry stopped him. A cry so tender, so full of recognition, so overflowing with perfect happiness, that Bion turned quickly with an involuntary smile.

The little fugitive stood before him, nude as on the night before, a little timid, but beaming, and awaiting only a gesture from him to throw herself into his arms and weep for joy.

"Thou! It is thou at last," she cried.

"I did not know where thou wouldst pass. I did not even know whether thou wouldst ascend the Nile. But I was sure that I would see thee again. I came here, and I waited. I divined well that thou wouldst turn away from the sun of the road and that thou wouldst go by the wood. Oh! How pleased I am! It seemed to me that three days passed while I waited . . . I am no longer . . . That which has come to me is so extraordinary . . ."

And she added, more sadly:

"Thou didst remain a long time with her."

Bion remained immobile and regarded her with some uneasiness.

"But, my little child, why didst thou come here?"

"What?" she cried. "I came to follow thee, to remain with thee always, always . . ."

"Thou comest to follow me, and yesterday, when thy father gave thee to me, thou didst flee like a foolish goat. I did not please thee last evening and I please thee this morning, for no reason? Thou hast singular whims."

The poor girl remained silent, then suddenly dissolved in tears, pressing her little nude, sob-racked body against a tree.

More than any other tiresome things, Bion detested touching scenes. With his finger, he tapped the child's shoulder and said:

"Farewell. Return to thy father's house. Thou wilt please him."

And he moved on, tranquilly.

But she ran after him. She grasped him by the mantle, by the arm, by the neck, and said quickly:

"I shall go where thou goest, I loved thee yesterday as I do today; I had never loved anyone; I love only thee, O, I shall love only thee . . . I went away, yesterday, because I was jealous of my sister, because I could not share thee with my sister nor love thee before her. If I had not fled, thou wouldst have taken me in passing and thou wouldst already have left me. After thee I would have given myself to another and to another, and so on until my marriage. Knowest thou that my sister has already known more strangers than I could tell thee in opening my two hands seven times? And I, also, should I have done that? Oh, I have felt

93

sure that, for all my life, I should belong to
the same man, to the first who should take
me. And this one are thou! Take me,
guard me always! I want to be thy wife
and to follow thee."

Bion, very much wearied, replied:

"My dear little one, thou reasonest like
a child. Thou sayest thyself that thou
hast never loved anyone, and I am well
convinced of it for, in the arms of her first
lover, a woman already dreams of her second and, in her heart, it is he whom she
loves. Thou wilt learn this a little later.

"There is no reason for always loving
the same man. Wouldst thou condemn
thyself to sleep all thy life under the same
roof? to wear always the same robe? to eat
always the same fruit? Love is not a sensation so very different from others, but

of all it is the most abundant: it is for this reason that it can be shared.

"The gods have spread upon thy mouth a love generous enough to satisfy an entire army. Thou hast no right to deprive others of the pleasure they hope for from thee. When thy sister shall marry, thou wilt remain alone in thy father's house: then there will still pass travelers who long since will have left their own hearth and the bed sacred to their marriage. Wearied by the sun and the length of the road, they will be refreshed by thine attentions. Thou wilt be able to conjure away their weariness and to leave, in their life, the remembrance of a happy hour.

"Thus, through the passage of the days, the diversity of loves, the promptness of farewells, thou wilt understand, little by

95

little, that one is not bound by love; and thou wilt more wisely choose the man to whom thou wilt give thy life."

"Could I ever choose better? Art thou not . . ."

"Oh, I am. I am without doubt the best, the only one, and thou art very certain of having found thy dream. Is it not this thou wert going to say? Ah well, see how thou hast deceived thyself, I should leave thee immediately afterwards, just as I left thy sister this morning. In the situation thou art in, it would be best for us to do nothing and to simply part. Thou didst make a deplorable choice. Try to forget it and go at once without turning thy head. In the House upon the Nile thou wilt find again thine afflicted father, the family hearth and the images of the

Gods. Thou wilt find again thine elder sister and she will teach thee that true virtue of which thou knowest only the semblance."

He kissed her on the cheek and resumed his walk between the trees. But he had not yet passed from sight beyond the great thickets of yellow flowers when, for the third time, he heard running steps and weeping behind him.

Then he became suddenly angry.

"I forbid thee to follow me!"

"I cannot leave thee. Do not drive me away. I do not ask to be a wife since thou refusest to love me. I beg thee, let me stay near thee. I shall belong to thee. Make anything of me. I will be thy slave, if thou wishest."

Bion coldly removed his girdle, wrapped

97

it like drawers around the child's loins, hung his filled sack, the gourd and the petasus upon her naked shoulder and in an indifferent voice:

"Go ahead," he said.

*
* *

This history caused some scandal and the women were not far from thinking that Bion was an abominable man. This was much worse when Rhea, who always wanted to know the final end of stories and the disposition of all the people, demanded:

"What happened afterward?"

For Clinias finished thus:

"Before the evening of the same day, Bion sold her, like a slave, to a wandering chief of the plains and he does not know what became of her."

98

The women were indignant, but Thrases was already speaking:

"That was his obvious right. Had she not said to him: "I belong to thee"? The characteristic of things which are owned is that they can be sold. There is nothing to say against it and, beside, she was a little fool whom he did well to pass over."

Melandryon was more severe:

"Reasons like that," he said, " are all too virtuous. Things cannot be judged by the relation of Good and Evil. These are considerations which vary according to climates, and of which the importance is much exaggerated. The single rule of life which seems legitimate is the love for beauty. If the child was pretty (Clinias omitted telling us this) Bion committed a grave fault in selling her to a stupid negro

99

who would disregard the charm of her form and the grace of her movements."

"She had a short nose," responded Clinias, "heavy lips and a brown skin."

"In that case," declared Melandryon, "he was not obliged to bother with her."

BYBLIS

or

The Enchantment of Tears

$\mathcal{A}ND$ Amaryllis, between the three young women and the three philosophers, related this fabulous allegory, as though to little children:

"Travelers whom I have known and who have been in Caria, having ascended the Meander much farther than any others had ever gone, have seen the God of the drowsy river, at the edge of the waters shadowed by rushes. He had a long, green beard and his face was wrinkled like the rocks on the gray banks from which hung weeping grasses. His ancient eyelids seemed dead upon eyes

103

forever blind. It is probable that those who would seek him today would no longer find him living.

"Now, it was he who was the father of Byblis, by his union with the nymph Cyanis; and I shall tell you the history of the unfortunate Byblis."

I

IN the original grotto from which the river mysteriously issued, the nymph Cyanis brought forth two children at one birth. One was a boy, whom she named Caunos; the other a girl, who was Byblis.

They grew up together on the banks of the Meander, and sometimes Cyanis showed them, under the light upon the surface, the divine appearance of their father whose spirit stirred the passing floods.

They knew nothing of the world be-

yond the forest where they were born.
They had never seen the sun except
through the network of the branches.
Byblis never left her brother, and put her
arm around his neck when they walked
together.

She wore a little tunic which her mother
had woven for her in the depths of the
water and which was blue and gray like
the first light of the dawn. Caunos wore
about his loins only a girdle of rushes from
which hung a yellow cloth.

When the day had brightened so that
they could walk in the wood, they would
go far away together, playing with fallen
fruits or searching for the largest flowers
and those with the best perfume. The
discoveries of one were always for the
other, and they did not quarrel, and be-

cause of this their mother praised them to
the other nymphs who were her friends.

Now, when twelve years had flown
away since the day of their birth, their
mother became uneasy and sometimes followed them.

The two children no longer played and,
after spending a whole day in the forest,
would return empty-handed, bringing
neither birds nor flowers nor fruits nor
garlands. They walked so closely together that their hair mingled. Byblis'
hands would wander over her brother's
arms. Sometimes she would kiss his
cheek; then they would both remain
silent.

When the heat was too great they
would creep in among the low branches

and there, lying upon their breasts on the fragrant moss, would talk together, admire each other and remain entwined.

Then Cyanis called her son aside and said:

"Why art thou sad?"

Caunos replied:

"I am not sad. In former times, I laughed and played. Now all is greatly changed. I have no need of games, mother, and, if I no longer laugh, it is because I am happy."

Cyanis asked:

"Why art thou happy?"

And Caunos replied:

"I look at Byblis."

And Cyanis asked farther:

"Why dost thou no longer care for the forest?"

"Because the hair of Byblis is softer than the grasses, and more perfumed; because the eyes of Byblis . . ."

But Cyanis stopped him:

"Child! Be silent!"

And, hoping to cure him of his forbidden passion, she took him at once to the dwelling of a mountain nymph who had seven daughters more marvelously beautiful than words could tell.

And both, concerting together, said to him:

"Choose. She who pleases thee Caunos, shall be thy wife."

But Caunos looked at the seven young girls with as indifferent an eye as though he saw seven rocks, for the image of Byblis alone filled all his little soul and he had no place in him for an unknown tenderness.

109

For a month, Cyanis conducted her son thus from mountain to mountain and from plain to plain, but without once succeeding in turning him from his desire.

At last, divining that she should never overcome this passionate obstinacy, she began to dislike her son and to accuse him of infamy. But the child did not at all understand why his mother reproached him. Why, among all women, should he be denied the very one he loved? Why should the tenderness which would be permitted in the importunate arms of another become criminal in the adored arms of Byblis? For what mysterious reasons should a feeling which he knew to be tender and good, capable of any sacrifice, be judged worthy only of every punishment? "Zeus," he thought, "had certainly espoused his sister; and Aphrodite Dionæa, with her brother Ares, had dared to deceive her brother Hephæstos." For he did not yet know that the gods had given intelligent morality only to themselves and that they troubled virtue with incomprehensible laws.

And Cyanis said to her son:

"I renounce thee as my child."

She beckoned to a centauress who was going toward the sea and made Caunos mount astride her.

The beast galloped away. For some time, Cyanis followed them with her gaze. Caunos, frightened, held f a s t to the shoulders, sometimes swallowed up by the masses of hair. The centauress galloped with long, powerful bounds; she fled in a straight line; she diminished in the green

111

distance. Soon she passed behind a clump of trees, then reappeared, but smaller, like a dot which hardly seemed to move. At last Cyanis could no longer distinguish her.

Slowly, Byblis' mother returned toward the forest.

She was sad, but proud also, at having saved, by a violent separation, the destinies of her two children; and she thanked the gods for having given her strength to accomplish the unpleasant duty.

"Now," she thought, "Byblis, left alone, will forget her sacrificed brother. She will become enamored of the first one who seeks to charm her and, perhaps, a line of demi-gods will issue from the bed of an

112

orderly marriage. Blessed are the immortal gods!"

But, when she returned to the grotto, little Byblis was no longer there.

II

WHEN Byblis found herself alone upon the little bed of green leaves where she lay, each night, beside her brother, she sought in vain for sleep; on this evening, the dreams would not visit her.

She arose; the night was sweet. A calm respiration slowly raised and lowered the profound masses of the forest. She seated herself upon a stone and gazed at the gliding water.

"Caunos," she thought, "Caunos. Why

115

has he not returned? What attracted him and what detains him? Why has my brother left me?"

And, while speaking these last words, she leaned over the spring . . .

"My father!" she repeated. "My father! Where is Caunos? Tell me. . ."

A murmur of the waters responded:

"Far . . ."

Byblis, frightened, resumed quickly:

"And when will he return? When will he return here?"

"Never . . ." replied the spring.

"Dead! He is dead!"

"No . . ."

"Where shall I find him?"

". . ."

The spring was silent. The light whispering of the reeds again became

116

monotonous. No divine appearance moved in the pure water.

Byblis raised herself, and ran. She knew by what path Caunos had departed with her mother. This was a narrow passage which wound among the trees and submerged itself in the forest. She did not often take it for it crossed a low ground which was infested with serpents and evil beasts. This time, her desire was stronger than her fear and she hurried on, trembling, at the best speed of her little, naked feet.

The night was not dark; but the shadows from the moon were black and, among the largest trees, Byblis had to feel her way.

She came to a place where the path divided. How should she know which road

117

to choose? Upon her knees, she searched
for a long time for a mark which would
guide her. The ground was dry. Byblis
could see nothing. But, as she raised her
head, she saw, hidden among the leaves of
an oak, a hamadryad with green breasts,
who watched her, smiling.

"Oh!" cried Byblis. "Which way did
he take? If thou didst see him, tell
me . . ."

The hamadryad extended one of her
long, branch-like arms toward the right,
and Byblis thanked her with a grateful
look.

Through that night, she walked for a
long time. The path continued always,
scarcely marked under the fallen leaves; it
advanced, winding always, according to
the ground and the trees, rising, descend-

ing, in the darkness, interminably.

At last, overcome by weariness, Byblis fell upon the moss, and slept.

On awakening, the next day, under a sun which was already high, she felt a strange softness along her extended hand. She opened her eyes; a yellow hind was licking it, slowly. But, at Byblis' first movement, the delicate animal bounded upon its slender hooves, raised its two ears, and fastened upon her its beautiful, humid eyes which were dark and gleaming like water among the rocks.

"Hind," said Byblis, "whose art thou? If thou belongest to the goddess Artemis, guide me, for I know her. At the full moon, I give her libations of goat's milk, and she knows it, hind, she loves me well.

119

If thou art one of her followers, deliver me from the anguish I suffer, and be sure thou wilt not displease the good Huntress of the Night."

The hind seemed to understand; she advanced, spacing her steps so that the child could follow her.

Together, they crossed, thus, a great part of the forest and also two brooklets which the hind leapt at a bound but which Byblis could pass only by entering water up to her knees. Byblis was full of confidence. She was sure, now, of being on the right road; without doubt, this hind had been sent by the goddess herself, in gratitude for her devotion; and the divine animal would guide her across the wood to the well-beloved brother whom she would never leave again. Each step brought nearer the time when she would see Caunos again. She already felt, against her breast, the affectionate embrace of the fugitive. A little of his breath seemed to have passed in the air and to have enchanted the cooling breeze.

Suddenly, the hind stopped, She slipped her young head between two young trees where, at the same time, appeared the horned profile of a stag; and, as though she had accomplished her desired end, she lay down, her hooves under her belly, and rested her chin upon the grass.

"Caunos!"

Byblis called.

"Caunos, where are thou?"

For her only reply, the stag made a few steps toward her, threatening her with his terrible horns which were twisted like ten

121

brown serpents   And then Byblis understood that the hind, like herself, had been
in search of her lover and that it is perhaps
useless to depend on the good offices of
those already fully absorbed by an intimate passion.

She turned back; but she was lost. She
took a new path which descended rapidly
toward an invisible valley. Her poor little
feet, wounded by the stones, torn by
roots, slipped on the brown carpet of pine
needles. At a turn of the irregular path,
which followed the course of a brook, she
paused before a divine couple. They were
two nymphs, of different essences; one of
them lived in the forests and the other in
the water of springs. The oread had
brought the naiad fresh offerings received

from the men, and they bathed together in the stream, undulating and enlaced.

"Naiad," said Byblis, "hast thou seen the son of Cyanis?"

"Yes. His shadow passed over me. It was yesterday, at sunset."

"From whence did he come?"

"I know not."

"Whither did he go?"

"I did not see."

Byblis gave a long sigh.

"And thou," she said, to the other nymph, "Hast thou seen the son of Cyanis?"

"Yes. Far from here, upon the mountain."

"From whence did he come?"

"I knew not."

"Whither did he go?"

"I have forgotten."

Then she added, raising herself amidst the rapid waters:

"Stay with us, young girl, stay. Why dost thou dream still of one who is no longer here? We have stored up for thee an infinity of present joys. There is no happiness in the future worth the trouble of pursuing it."

But Byblis did not at all believe that the nymph had spoken well. Although she could not express the ideas of her little soul, she could conceive of no other joy than the suffering of persevering in her search for happiness. During the first day of her useless journey, she had counted on the aid and the zeal of unknown people. Since she had seen them heedless of assist-ing her purpose she no longer depended on any but herself   And, leaving the winding path, she penetrated at hazard into the labyrinth of the wood.

Meanwhile, the two immortals repeated their wise words:

"Stay with us, young girl, stay. Why dost thou dream still of one who is no longer here. There is no happiness in the future worth the trouble of pursuing it."

And, long, long after, the child, always climbing the mysterious mountain, heard in the distance two clear voices calling together:

"Byblis!"

III

FOR a night and a day, Byblis walked over the mountain. She anxiously questioned all the divinities of the woods, those of the trees, those of the glades and those of the shadowy caverns. She related her sorrow with interminable confidences, she supplicated, she trembled, she wrung her little hands. But no one had seen Caunos.

She had mounted so far that the sacred name of her mother was no longer known

127

where she passed, and the indifferent nymphs did not understand what she was trying to say.

She wished to retrace her steps, but she had lost herself. On all sides, a confused colonnade of enormous pines surrounded her. There were no more paths. There was no horizon. She ran aimlessly. She called desperately.

There was no longer even an echo.

Then, as her weary eyelids were closing, little by little, she lay down upon the ground, and a passing dream said to her, in a slow voice:

"Thou wilt never see him again, thy brother; thou wilt never see him again."

She awakened with a start.

Her hands stretched out, her mouth

128

opened, but with such anguish that she had not the strength to cry out.

The moon had risen, red like blood behind the tall black lines of the pines. Byblis could scarcely see it. It seemed to her that a moist veil had spread itself over her long eyes. An eternal silence slumbered in the wood.

And then a swollen tear filled the corner of her left eye

Byblis had never wept. She believed that she was going to die, and she sighed as though a divine relief mysteriously assisted her.

The tear spread, trembled, enlarged; then suddenly rolled over her cheek.

Byblis remained motionless, her eyes fixed, before the moon.

129

And then a swollen tear filled the corner of her right eye. It enlarged like the first, slipped through the lashes, and fell.

Two other tears were born, two burning drops which left damp lines on her cheeks. They came to the corners of her mouth; a delicious bitterness enervated the dejected child.

So, never again should her hand touch the affectionate hand of Caunos. Never again should she see the shadowy glow of his gaze, his dear head and his young hair. Never again should they sleep, side by side, entwined upon the same bed of leaves. The forests no longer knew his name.

An outburst of despair dropped Byblis' face into her hands; but such an abund-

130

ance of tears wet her burning cheeks that she felt as though a miraculous spring was bearing away all her sufferings, like dead leaves upon the water of a torrent.

The tears were born gently within her, mounted to her eyes, floated, overflowed, and, gliding in a warm sheet over her cheeks, inundated her narrow breast and fell upon her close-joined legs. She no longer felt them rounding, one by one, between her long eyelids: they had become a smooth, continuous stream, an inexhaustible flow, the effusion of an enchanted water.

Meanwhile, awakened by the moonlight, the immortals of the forest had hastened up from all sides. The bark of the trees had become transparent, revealing the forms of the nymphs, and even the shivering naiads, leaving their waters and their rocks, had poured into the wood.

They pressed about Byblis, calling to her, frightened, for the course of the child's tears had marked, in the earth, a deep sinuous line which moved slowly toward the plain.

But already Byblis no longer heard anything, neither voices, nor steps, nor the night-wind. Little by little, her posture became eternal. Under the flood of tears, her skin had taken the smooth, white tint of marble bathed by the waters. The wind no longer disturbed her hair lying along her arms. She had died away into pure stone. A shadowy light still lingered

faintly in her vision. Suddenly, this went out; but the fresh tears still ran unceasingly.

*

* *

"*It was thus that Byblis was changed into a fountain.*"

DANAE

or

Sorrow

𝒯HE day was beautiful.

The sadness left by the story of the night before had vanished with the mist; the women ran in the wood; there were bursts of laughter upon the road.

The exuberance of Spring bent the branches of the trees and made the fields overflow along the narrow paths. The outspread flowers, grazed in passing, left yellow marks on the edge of the tunics. A sea of violets bathed the feet of the cedars: there the young people lay down in a group.

137

And, *as the hour had come to people the deserted forest with fabulous personages, Rhea, a straightforward young girl, for whom words had no profound sense, thought to express the desire of all by demanding of Thrases* "a story about happiness."

"Yes, yes," *cried Lampito.*

But Amaryllis exclaimed:

"No! oh no! not that, above all! One should not speak of happiness. He who tells of his happiness, abandons it, word by word. He who tells of the happiness of others, augments his own sadness. It is a story of sorrow which I shall tell you today. Unhappiness sows the seed of pity, which is gentle and beneficent. In the unhappiness of Danae each of you shall recognize your own, and you shall become happy at the memory of lost sorrows."

Without replying, the others made a circle about her and she continued thus:

DANAE

Although there was neither mist nor
mist she hurried along twilight, or
low barge...and with raven-wings of
love...for some time to unravel it to
their wine coast, remained toward the
From Danae, I think she was quite

I

WHEN Danae, the mother of Perseus, left the Argonian shores, she remained for a long time at the stern, watching the land gradually recede and the stretch of waters increase.

Her father had placed her, naked, in a long, black boat with her new-born child, and two little funereal oboli, so that she could pay her own and her son's passage on *that other* boat when the night of death should have filled their eyes, through famine, cold, or the tossings of the sea.

141

Although there was neither mast nor sails, the wind hurried along the light, hollow barge. A gull with curved wings followed it for some time in uncertain flight, then, wing-weary, returned toward the land.

Then Danae felt that she was quite alone, and, her hands over her eyes, she dissolved in tears.

But she did not weep long, for she had a simple soul into which sorrow had not yet entered. The little voice of her child made her turn, already smiling. She took the baby in her arms, lay down on her back on a woolen rug which covered the bottom of the boat and began to play.

She held the child like a wax doll, she amused herself with his great round eyes, his toothless mouth which tried to speak, the rosy folds of his wrists, and his nails which were so tiny that they might have been taken for the wings of flies.

With a quick movement, she nearly stifled him in her arms, she caressed his bald little head, his little legs, his little doubled-up feet; she made him walk upon her, jump, run, fall, roll. She enveloped him in her hair, and, with a finger on his lip, she made him laugh.

"Listen," she said to him, at last. "I will relate thy history."

It was not probable that the child could understand. However, he was of a divine race and nothing was impossible for those born of the great Olympians.

And she spoke thus:

"I am Danae, the daughter of Acrisios who is king over the land of Argos. My mother is the wise Eurydice, and I have no brother with winged arrows, and I have no sisters with ringlets of violets.

"I remember having played, when I was a little girl, on the banks of the Inachos, where Artemis was said to bathe, and in the forests of the Artemision where she hunted the yellow hinds. I had friends; I had slaves; when I passed in the streets, women stretched out their hands toward me. Then, suddenly, I was imprisoned, and I could no longer see either the water or the earth.

"I was imprisoned in a tower of bronze, so high that I could not hear even the uproar of the festivals of Dionysos. And the ceiling of my chamber was made of brazen bars, between which I could see the sky.

"And it was there that I grew up, alone with my nurse, between the sky and the rugs. I lived there for so long that I forgot the earth and the wind among the trees and the color of the water. I saw only the sky; but what cannot one see in the changing sky? In the morning, when I awakened, it was like a red curtain strewn with little green flowers. The clouds were born, passed, floated, mingled or scattered. Sometimes, before they disappeared, I gave them names; but they were the friends of a moment and, like a cup of wine thrown into a river, they dissolved in the rapid wind. Behind them, the sky was very clear and, around the sun, almost white or perhaps of a color for which I had no name: the color of light."

145

The baby began to wail. She rocked him. He became silent.

"In the evening, there was a great sea of purple in which the outspread clouds bathed themselves, like beautiful women with long hair and yellow scarfs. At night, there were the stars.

"It was from above, it was from the distant sky, that there descended into me the mysterious rain . . ."

She closed her eyes and smiled gently, invaded by an idle remembrance. When she opened them again, the child was asleep. So she did not tell any more, she did not tell how her inexplicable pregnancy had suddenly reawakened the senile fears of Acrisios to whom a diviner had predicted that he should die at the hand

146

of his grandson; she did not tell how, for forty weeks, she had felt growing within her the fruit of that marvelous love; nor how, with the child born into the world, the king now exposed them, she and he, to death by famine, by cold or by the tossings of the sea.

However, need she think of that? Had not the supernatural influence, which had brought about the birth of Perseus, saved her from the first peril and was it not one's duty to always submit to the majesty of the gods?

The child, awakening, moved his arms and began to cry. She recalled that she had not nursed him since morning. She bent over him and gave him her breast. The heat was overwhelming; Danae feared that the strong light would trouble

147

the poor little person, and, for the second time, she covered his face with her thick, soft hair.

Time rolled on, slowly — Argos and Tiryns had disappeared. To the right and to the left, the shores of the gulf, stretched to the horizon, were vaguely blended with the floating mists. In the distance a swift dolphin shot clear of the water, plunging in again head first. Sometimes green sea-wrack wrapped itself around the prow, its two ends threading out in a doubled wake. Danae detached it with her hand, wondering whether the wet strands which she held between her fingers had not served as a coronal on the forehead of some sea god.

Evening came. There were no sails upon the sea. The sun was eclipsed by a

148

resplendent cloud from which arose a wide shaft of light which seemed to issue from the waters. An immense shadow hid the Mediterranean. The waves softened as though overtaken by drowsiness. The little boat scarcely moved: Danae was not sure that it had not stopped. . . . Then the wind fell, suddenly.

Danae, who had laid down the child, took him up in her arms to nurse him again. But she had forgotten that she herself had taken no nourishment since morning. Her milk was nearly exhausted: the child began to cry.

She looked at him, then at her breasts, and at the sea. Nothing about the sea frightened her except the silence; she shivered. On all the horizon she saw no living thing. It seemed that the world had disappeared and that she was forever alone. She dipped her hand in the water: even the water was motionless.

She wished to sing, but she no longer recognized her voice and she was suddenly silent.

Then she wept: she stretched out in the bottom of the boat where she could see only the changing sky, as in her room in the tower. And thus she fell asleep.

II

NIGHT ascended in the west, like a blue vapor. The stars appeared faintly, here and there, like little drops. The sea had become so calm that it reflected the uncertain glimmer, and the little boat seemed suspended in the center of a celestial sphere.

Then the mirror was disturbed and, if Danae had not been asleep, she would without doubt have trembled with fright. A hand had come out of the water.

It was not like the hands of the women of earth, for it was blue on the back and the palm was the color of gold, as though it had caressed the sun plunged beneath the sea.

The hand lifted and grasped the edge of the boat; the entire arm appeared and, soon, floating on the water, the first ringlets of green hair; then the watery eyes and the mouth and the glistening body emerged. And it was soft-cheeked Pherusa, one of the divine Nereids.

She took the child in her arms, not to steal him away but to save his life, for she placed between his lips the extended tip of her cool breast, and the child drank and was satisfied.

And after her there appeared the perfect Evagora, not less beautiful and with equally graceful hands and arms, born, like her of old Nereus and the fair-haired

Doris. She held in her hand a swaddling-band of bright purple with which she clothed the little person, so that the deadly breath of the night should not descend until the hour fixed in the shadowy dwellings beneath the earth.

After these, arose kind Antonoë who, in her turn took the child and cradled him upon the waters. Then Nossa and Cymothoë, Actinia and Protomedia, all four irreproachable; and these bore with them from the depths of the abyss, a bowl, so wide and so shining that the hardiest divers have never seen anything comparable to it. And Psamathis appeared, she also, Psamathis of the transparent hands, and Melita of the green nails and Thalia of the red ears. And they took up the sleeping Danae and laid her in the wide-spread-ing bowl upon a bed of soft sea-wrack and flowers from beneath the sea. And Protia who surpassed all her sisters in swimming, and Eucrata of the tender lips, and Saia, who blew the conch-shell and Speia, who pursued the dolphins, pulled down the stern of the boat so that the sterile sea entered and, with a swirl, swallowed it up. Then all the other Nereids emerged suddenly: Eratia, who threw upon the sea the petals of the rose of twilight, Eunica, whose hair under the water checked the swift ships, Amphitrite, whose bright eyes appeared in the hollows of green waves, Galenis, who could smooth out the billows, Pontoporia, who agitated the waters, Nesais, who appeared as an island to the voyagers from the west, Themistia, who carried away the star Iryllis and put

154

it in a ring for her white toe, Cymatolegia, who gathered and drank the frothy foam, Lysianassa, who ruled over the shadowy depths of the ocean, Hippothoë, who let the black ships pass between her naked legs without being touched by the highest masts, and Doris and Halimeda, who held each other by the hand, Evarne of the long eye-lashes and light-fingered Agava.

When they were all united together, like a great cloud floating about the moon-like bowl, the Old Man of the Sea appeared before them: this was Nereus, crowned with sea-wrack, the immortal who had generated this charming race of Goddesses.

He made a sign, and the procession of his daughters followed him; and, floating in their midst, carried along the bowl, filled with glaucous light, where white Danae slept with the infant Perseus, saved from the inexorable waters.

And the appearance of divine figures continued unendingly. Proteus emerged, with his monstrous seals born of the beautiful Halosydnis; Atlas, who was to be vanquished by the child; Thaumas, the dazzling husband of Electra—father of the cerulean Iris and of the three virgin Harpies; Ino-Leucothea, who suffered immortality for love of her son, Melicertes; Glaucos, who loved Scylla; Charybdis, dangerous to sailors; and Phorcys, god of storms and of death upon the sea.

And the most terrible of these gods became quiet, as they led, toward the shore, the young woman enveloped in her dream. The dusky throng of the Tritons,

with heavy-lipped mouths and calloused
hands, swam more gently than a school of
little fish. They had stuffed the twisted
mouths of their conch-shells with sea-
weed so that even the breeze of morning
would not vibrate in a distant rumor; and
they advanced cautiously as though they
feared to disturb the sea. But the wake
of this multitude stretched out to the two
horizons.

III

When Danae returned to herself, her child was cradled in her arms and she her-self lay upon a royal bed of purple byssus. At her first questions, she was told that the divinities of the sea had brought her to the Isle of Seriphos where Polydectes had recently become king, and that she was in his palace.

She lived there, bringing up her son, spinning wool and gathering roses. Her

159

life was happy and uneventful. To remain faithful to the memory of the Gold, she had refused the hand of the king. She talked with no one except her old nurse who had come from Argos to rejoin her and who never left her.

The child grew. Twelve years rolled by. He had been given a bow and arrows, and a small, sharp sword. After that, he passed all his days in the chase, alone, and sometimes became lost in the vast forest peopled with beasts, some of which were divine. He accomplished miraculous killings in those sombre thickets.

One evening, he returned, running, wet with perspiration and spotted with blood; two goat's feet protruded from his quiver. When he saw Danae, he cried:

"A good hunt, mother! I ran in the

160

wood all day, pursuing this insolent little satyr who, the day before yesterday, mocked my bare lip and my pale legs. I followed his tracks in the damp earth and on the rocks scratched by his hooves; and I met him at the entrance of his cave. I threw my bow among the branches and we struggled, body to body. He was vigorous, mother; I smothered in his clasp. But I seized my bundle of arrows and, with one thrust, I plunged them into his lean side. He gave a great cry and fell upon the grass like a wounded boar. Then I cut off his two hooves and I bring them to thee as a trophy."

Danae shuddered at the child's impiety, and the old nurse hid her eyes, for she saw, in this senseless act, the presage and notice of a great misfortune to come. And, in fact, the fatal event arrived on the following day.

Danae had the enjoyment of all the gardens, all the palace, all the riches of Polydectes, except one path, one door, one small vault.

For long years, she had reflected on the perpetual interdiction of this one point of the earth, and she had ended by imagining that the little closed vault held, for him alone, all the happiness she did not possess, all the unknown joys which she desired more than life.

On that following day, she penetrated the path.

She opened the door.

She descended the first flight of stairs.

The second.

To the bottom.

Her nurse hastened after her. She cried: "Danae! Danae! Thou dost wrong to come here. Do not descend, Danae. Thou hast been protected, thou knowest well. Why wilt thou do that from which thou art protected? There is but one place in the world where thou shouldst not go, and it is that which thou wouldst see . . . Thou wouldst not go out, thou wouldst not leave thy chamber except when the sun had set or when a storm thundered. Yet thou wouldst not go to other cities. No one ever saw thee in the fields. Thou wouldst never have come here, thou wouldst never have wished to, if I had not told thee that Polydectes would protect thee. Why did I tell thee that? Why did I speak when thou didst ask nothing? I am sure that this will react against thee. Still

once more, hear me, Danae. I know why
one would protect thee from what thou
wouldst do today. I could not tell thee,
but I know, I know, I know! It is concerned with thy happiness, I swear to
thee by thy lovely hair which I saw
lengthen, by thy lovely eyes which I often
put to sleep, by thy lovely mouth which
I nourished when thou wast naked in my
arms like a little waxen Eros. Danae!
Danae! Do not descend these steps, do not
enter this vault, do not open the doors
here, do not touch the locks nor turn the
keys of bronze! It is thine unhappiness
which is there: it is the sorrow of thy life.
When one knows one's sorrow, it should
be forever forgotten! When one knows
it not, one should not search for it. Danae!
return, put out thy lamp, return to the

day, go away from here, never return here, never think of it. Here thou goest toward death, here thou goest toward the night . . ."

Danae spoke, in a slow voice:

"The oil has spilled upon my hands. It has fallen upon my naked foot. I tremble. Dost thou see, nurse? Take my lamp, I can no longer carry it. Oh! I am all covered with perfume. I should have poured it all upon my hands. But we have need of the lamp. Light me, nurse."

The nurse wept:

"She enters; it was her destiny that she should enter. It was her destiny that she should be unfortunate. Have pity on us, merciful gods!"

And Danae replied:

"I know something of what is behind

165

this door. Sorrow, that is always the same thing. *It is a by-gone happiness which cannot be renewed . . .*"

And she continued, as though in a dream:

"What happiness have I ever had to equal this one? I know well what is coming. That is to say . . . I do not know all, but I divine something of it. Raise the light higher, nurse. I am going to open the door."

"This is not even the door of a tomb. It is something even more horrible . . . It is . . . oh! I cannot tell thee. Thou shalt see it, Danae. It is thy destiny, as thou thyself canst see. No one can prevent thee. Thou couldst not prevent thyself from going in here."

"The door is not heavy. The hinges are

166

smooth. It must be often opened, this door, is it not? How is it that anyone is so much concerned with my misfortune, when it appears as nothing to him? Or better; perhaps it is a misfortune for me alone and a happiness for all others.—The door gives way. I barely touched it with the tip of my finger and felt it turn itself . . . Seest thou, now, seest thou? Seest thou? . . ."

A pile of gold pieces rolled about her, through the wide opened door. She gave a frightened cry:

"Ah! . . . Zeus . . . oh! oh! oh! . . . My lover!"

She threw herself upon the ground, in the out-pouring treasure.

"Alas! Alas!" said the nurse. "Alas! It has come."

Danae had thrown aside her tunic, her girdle, her embroidered ribbons.

"Adored Zeus! Beloved Zeus! Gentle Zeus! Then I meet thee again and, as before, in a prison of bronze. It was thee they concealed in this subterranean night, thunder-hurtling God! Since I was free, it was thee they wished to wall up, while I died in the sunlight, ignorant of the hiding place of thy splendor through which Perseus was magnified in my womb! Lover! Lover! I am here! Awaken! Quicken thyself! Arise! I am Danae! Danae! . . ."

And she rolled herself upon the icy metal.

"Thou dost not hear me?. . . Oh! how cold thou art! My hands seem plunged into snow . . . Ah! . . . Ah! . . . it falls

back . . . it no longer knows me. This is not he, nurse! . . . Tell me that this is not he . . . I had well divined this which has happened . . . I cannot see any more . . . My arms pain me . . . ."

"Come, Danae," said the nurse. "Come, thou shouldst go up at once. We should not remain any longer here."

*
* *

Amaryllis ended.

There was a moment of silence; then an exclamation of disappointment from Rhea.

"And is that all?" *she cried.* "Thou art worse than Melandryon! What happened to her? Why did she say that her arms pained her?"

169

"Hast thou forgotten," said Amaryllis, "how Melandryon said that symbols were not to be explained."

"But . . ."

"I do not think that story was so very sorrowful," Philinna interposed. "It seems to me that Danae was fortunate. At the most, she was disappointed when she found the gold so cold; but, on the other hand, had she expected such happiness, up to that moment? Had she expected to ever see the golden shower again and to feel, through it, the living embrace of the god?"

"But certainly," said Rhea, "thou didst not mean to infer that she was dying. For we know that she lived in Argos with Perseus, long afterward, when he reigned there, after he had accidentally killed King Acrisios in fulfillment of the prophecy."

"If thou knowest that," said Melandryon, "or believest it to thine own satisfaction, why dost thou question? It was Amaryllis' story and she ended it, doubtless, according to her thought. Interpret it as thou wilt. As for me, I am more interested at this moment in the cool water of yonder spring."

SUPPLEMENT

*T*HOSE who have read Pierre Louÿs' Spanish romance, "Woman and Puppet," know that this Author could give to a modern theme the same interest he bestowed by preference on the antique. He could also, on occasion, blend the two.

Of the two following pieces, "Spring Night" is taken from "Archipel," a volume of travel-sketches published in 1906. "A New Pleasure" was first published in 1899 and later incorporated in "Sanguines."

SPRING NIGHT

I

WRAPPED in her light cloak, behind the gate of the garden, Nephelis sat waiting.

Under the trees, the night was so profound that she could not see her hand before her eyes, and only the fragrance of the trees revealed their hidden presence. All slept, the men far off, the birds hidden, the interwoven branches invisible. The silence of the earth was as pure as the blackness of the shadows. Nephelis sat motionless, her hands clasped over her knee, her head on one side.

She did not wish to move. Unaccustomed, as a wife, to the artifices of seductions, she did not stir a fold of her cloak, for fear lest the perfumes of her body might be lost in the air stirred by the movement. And, knowing well that she had come too soon, she waited patiently, satisfied at being there, intoxicated with hope.

Gently, a finger tapped the outside of the door.

Already!

Noiselessly, she removed the heavy bar and opened the door on its oiled hinges. She heard a step on the path, but saw nothing except the black night.

"Do not look for me," she murmured. "I

178

am here. I will precede thee; come quickly;
I am afraid of the slaves, lest one of them
see us. Follow me. Beyond the thickets,
thou wilt be able to see my shadow."

She walked on tip-toe. Her little sandals
barely touched the sand or the mosaic
pavement. A branch, which she grazed,
made her shudder. There was a furtive
rustling through the vast silence, and the
stirring flowers threw out their perfume.

The first, she entered the chamber, ran
to a niche where she had put a screen over
an earthen lamp to veil, without extin-
guishing, it; and, when she had released a
little of the light, she turned.

"Gods!" she cried, "Gods! Gods! Gods!
It is not he!"

The man had advanced to the center of

the floor. She recoiled toward the wall until her back struck it heavily, and her hands wandered uncertainly over its surface.

"Who art thou?"

"I am not *he*, as thou hast said. Art thou quite sure of that? There is a *he*, is there not, and the rest of the world? I, I am the rest, humanity, the crowd, of which nothing is wanted."

Nephelis regarded him, almost fainting. He was a bony man, hairy and bearded, his heavy beard accenting his leanness. His head seemed made of hair. Four teeth were missing from his upper jaw, so that his moustache fell mingling with his beard, and this detail was horrible. His thin neck projected from a cloak of wool which was sufficiently dirty and fantastically draped. His legs appeared shorter than his body. He was neither large, nor small, but the lamp, set on the ground, doubled his body in an immense shadow, half on the wall and half on the ceiling.

He crossed his arms violently and thrust his hands under his arm-pits.

"Aha!" he exclaimed. "The perfumed bed! rose petals! an amphora of cool wine! Someone was expected, even though that one was not me. When the husband makes war, the wife has a debauch. Ha! Ha! Coronals of flowers! . . . But I smell myrrh, which nauseates me . . . And this lamp with its black smoke . . . That smacks of prostitution in thy house, dost thou hear me? . . . Hello! Take off thy robe and

181

practice thy business! Here is a drachma."

Shooting across the chamber, the piece of silver struck Nephelis in the belly. She stifled a cry.

"Miserable one," she said, in a thin voice, "Thou shalt know what it will cost thee to speak thus to me. Yes, I have a husband, and I have a lover, but the door of the garden has opened again; my lover is there, in the passage; he is coming; he approaches; and if he finds thee here he will kill thee like a worm."

"He will kill me?" said the unknown. "How will he do that? I have been dead these hundred years. Thou askest my name? I am the King of Egypt, embalmed."

Nephelis passed her hand slowly over her face, feeling a cold chill of fear . . .

182

"I am lost," she exclaimed. "He is mad."

The man, seeing her pale, resumed, smiling:

"Do not cry out, my pretty friend, or I will kill thee; and for thee, who hast not yet died, this will mean more than it would to a corpse like mine. Look at my mummied flesh."

With an abrupt movement, he threw off his vestments and appeared nude.

"Thou didst just say that the gate had opened again. That is impossible. The bar is in place. No one is in the garden, no one in the passage. Practice thy business, my girl, I have given thee a drachma. And do not cry out or, by Zeus, I will slay thee at once."

At that instant, Nephelis would have

welcomed death. Her fright far surpassed that which the dead feel at the sight of the eternal Lethe . . . But death by this man—Oh! what could be worse!

She did not cry out.

With a supreme effort, knowing that the insane should not be contradicted, she breathed out a few phrases, painfully articulated by her dry, cold tongue:

"Yes, thou art King of Egypt . . . thou art covered with little bands . . . But it is beneath thy dignity, Lord, to remain in the house of thy servant . . . Shall I show thee the path? . . . Thy queens, fairer than women, sing at the gates of the garden."

The madman started.

"King! King! Nonsense! Who said I was a king? Do I look like a man? Is it not

184

evident that I am a god? And how could I have entered here, poor fool, if I had not been a god? The door is locked; I told thee, the bar is in its sockets. I did not enter by the door. I am the emanation of that black amphora. I am Bacchus! Bacchus! Bacchus!"

He clamped the coronal of roses on his head and began to dance wildly.

Imperceptibly, Nephelis slipped along the wall, seeking to reach a place from which she could take flight. The madman saw nothing, spinning around in the intoxication of his bacchanal; but, as she stooped toward the lock, she felt a bony hand descend upon her shoulder. For the first time, he touched her. She recoiled once more to the depths of the chamber.

185

"Ah!" he exclaimed, pausing, "Thy skin is fresh, my girl. Why art thou not disrobed? Take off thy robe! I have paid thee."

He walked toward her and drew the loose, thin robe away from one of her breasts.

Nephelis flattened herself against the wall. She tried to speak, but not a word came from her trembling, frightened lips . . . The madman's fingers grasped the admirable breast and pressed it: a thin jet of milk spirted out.

At the sight of this, he paled. His voice changed and became like that of a little child.

"Mamma," he cried, "Mamma! Why hast thou not nursed me, these hundred years? What have I done that thou shouldst give thy breast to another, to another whom thou awaitest in a bed of roses and perfumes? Is it because I no longer have teeth, that thou wilt not nurse me? Mamma! Why hast thou left me?"

And, holding with his hands the despairing Nephelis' arms, he quickly set his lips to the nipple and sucked it thirstily.

A start of horror straightened the chest of the young woman.

"Monster! It is my child's milk thou drinkest!"

She shook herself free and grasped the man by the throat; but, in an instant, she was subdued.

"Ha! Ha!" he cried. "I told thee no one could kill a dead person. On the other hand, thou shalt see that it is easy to kill a living woman . . . Ha! Ha! No! Do not cry out. I will not slay thee. This is a game; it is a festival. Give me thy hair-ribbon."

He tore the band from her long hair which fell silently, and, seizing from behind Nephelis' two wrists, he bound them tightly upon her loins.

The young woman's teeth chattered. Once more, she wished to cry out, but a last hope sustained her . . . The garden door had not been closed . . . *He* was coming, the lover, the saviour; *he* would deliver her . . . Ah! how she wished for him! In what a desperate burst, all the energy of her desire strained toward him!

Meanwhile, the madman had removed

her girdle and detached the clasp and silver buckle on her right shoulder. Her vestment sank down. In vain Nephelis closed her knees. The man snatched away the robe and, grasping the unfortunate girl about the waist, threw her upon the bed where she fell, moaning.

A breath of perfumes mounted from the shaken couch.

"Ah! That smell of myrrh!" the madman cried again. "Thy kennel is infected, daughter of joy! Ha! Out with the myrrh! Down with it! Down with it! . . . I am Psammetichus, son of the Sun. Myrrh is the odor of the Night. I am the conquering King, the Highest, the King! the King! Myrrh is the odor of filthy caverns. Out with the myrrh, daughter of the Night! By

189

the horns of Hathor and by the jaws of Pasht! Down with it! Down with it! Down with it!"

He subsided, his head bent.

Nephelis, cowering at the extremity of the couch, watched him, wide-eyed.

A great calm followed. The man was silent. Outside, the same nocturnal peace brooded over the deserted garden. Then *he* was not coming! Gods! Perhaps *he* had come, *he* had knocked, *he* had not passed the door, *he* had gone . . . gone . . . A cruel anguish contracted Nephelis' breast.

And the madman recovered himself.

"Thou art beautiful," he said, softly. "How long hast thou been my wife? Thou wert not like this when I was king. Thy blond hair has become black. Thy narrow

190

flanks have become larger . . . And thy legs! . . . Oh! thy legs are very large! . . . Open them! . . ."

He continued talking to her, resting his hand on a marble tabouret which held vials of perfumes.

"Fear nothing," he said. "I am old. Thou seest, my girl, I am an old man . . . I have been dead an hundred years. Do not turn away from a mummy. I wish only to kiss thy mouth, and to sleep, to sleep upon thy breast, oh mother."

He advances his bony hands slowly, as though imploring her. But a nervous spasm shook him from head to foot. He leapt upon the bed, over the young woman and fell on the other side.

"Aaaah!"

At last she had cried out! A cry long

like an agony, a rending of her whole soul, a despairing plaint for rescue, to the gods, for a miracle, for life!

"Help! Help!" screamed the madman. "Stop struggling, daughter of the Night! Do not close thy teeth so, my kiss shall penetrate thee! Ha! the myrrh! the myrrh! Thou shalt conceive, be sure! Stars issue from thy breast like bees from a hive! Ha! ha! ha! ha! ha! For I am old . . ."

Nephelis had freed her right hand and, with a movement so quick that the madman saw nothing, she seized a heavy object from the tabouret and struck him on the temple.

She drew herself upright on the bed, her mouth open, her hands before her face, with a sort of laughter more frightful than any moaning. The man had fallen under

192

the blow but, for her, he was not dead. She seized quickly, from a slender vase, her long hair-pins, ten or twelve sharp points of which any one would be mortal and, twenty times, she plunged them all into his lean chest, between his projecting ribs, into his stomach, abdomen, eyes and cheeks.

And when the slaves, awakened by her cries, hurried in, they found her trampling upon the corpse, covered with blood, entirely naked and with her hands raised toward the sky, like an impossible Andromeda who had triumphed over the Monster.

27 December 1905.

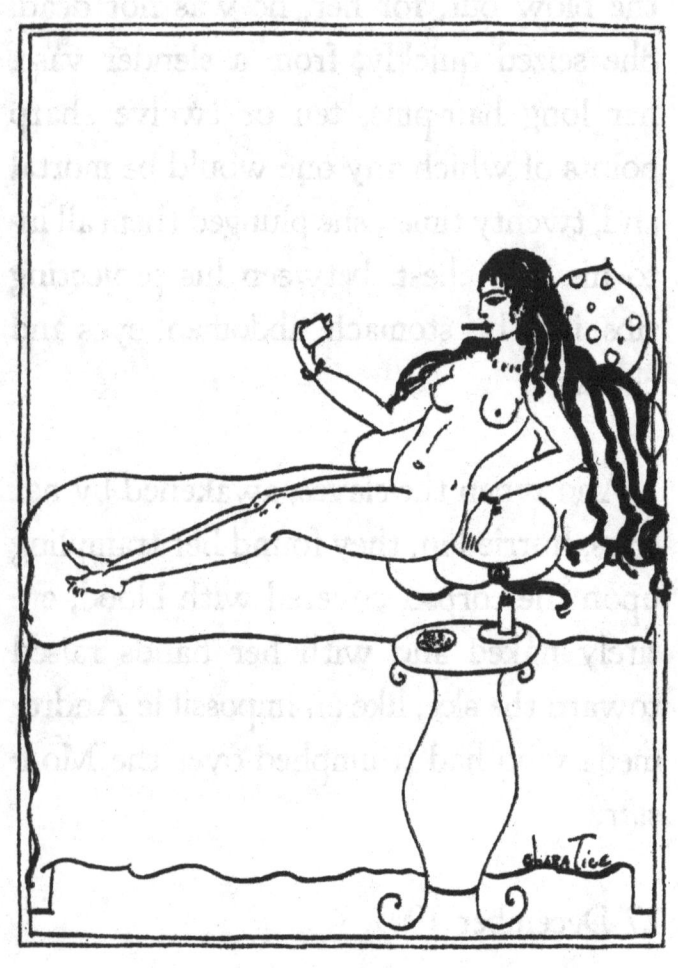

A NEW PLEASURE

I

FOUR or five years ago, I occupied, several days a week, a small, but quiet and well furnished ground floor, in a street which communicated at one end with the little Monceau Park. This fact had no interest for me, for the gate was always closed in the evening before midnight, so that I could not walk there precisely at the hour when I most enjoyed the open air.

One night as I found myself at home, in silent conversation with two blue pottery

cats crouched upon a white table, I hesitated between two ways of whiling away
the solitude: writing a sonnet and smoking
cigarettes, or smoking cigarettes and gazing at the ceiling.

The important thing is always to have
a cigarette at hand; it surrounds objects
with a delicate, celestial tint which softens
lights and shadows, effaces sharp angles
and, by a perfumed sorcery, casts over the
restless spirit a variable balance from
which it can fall into dreams.

This evening, I had the intention to
write and the desire to do nothing; in
other words, the evening seemed likely to
resemble many others, fated to end before
a virgin sheet of paper and an ash-tray full
of cadavers, when I was drawn from my
thoughts by an unexpected ring at the bell.

I raised my head. I satisfied myself that, on Friday the ninth of June, I expected no one at this hour of the night; but, when a second ring followed closely on the first, I went to the door and drew the lock.

Opening the door, I saw a woman.

She was enveloped in a flowing cloak which was of woolen cloth like a traveler's cloak, but woven in figures like a ball wrap. This was closed about her neck with a tufted roll of chenille from which her head barely emerged, brown under her blond tinted hair. Her face was young, sensual, a little mocking; two eyes very dark, a mouth very red.

"Will thou permit me to enter?" she asked, inclining her head upon her shoulder.

I drew back with the singular astonishment of a man who sees entering his house, at an hour when one scarcely receives even the most intimate friends, a woman of whom he could not recall the least memory and who, with her first words, addressed him with a familiar "thou."

"Dear friend," I said timidly, when I had followed her into my room, "Dear friend, do not blame me; I recognize thee perfectly but by some misfortune I cannot at the moment recall thy name. Is it Lucien? or Tototte?"

She smiled indulgently and, without responding, removed her cloak. Her robe was of water-green silk, ornamented with enormous irises woven into the cloth itself, the stems ascending along the body to the low, square-cut opening which left exposed the tops of her breasts. She wore on each arm a little golden serpent with emerald eyes. A necklace of large pearls in two rows shone upon her dark skin, marking the base of her neck which was rounded and mobile.

"If thou dost recognize me," she said, "it is because thou has seen me in some dream. I am Callisto, the daughter of Lamia. For eighteen hundred years my tomb remained in peace in the flowery woods of Daphne, near the hills where once was voluptuous Antioch. But now the tombs have traveled. I was carried away to Paris and my shadow followed the stone which contained my fragile ashes. For a long time after, I slept in the glacial caverns of the Louvre. I might have remained there forever, if a noble pagan, a holy man, M.

Louis Menard, the only one who, today
remembers the rites and divine ceremonies,
had not pronounced before my tomb the
traditional words which return to the
poor dead an ephemeral and nocturnal
life. For seven hours each night I can walk
in thy squalid city . . ."

"Oh! Poor girl!" I interrupted. "How
changed thou must find the world!"

"Yes and no. I find the houses dark, the
costumes ugly and the sky dismal; (what
singular idea causes you to live in such a
climate!) I find life is more senseless and
the people have a less happy air; but if I
have been surprised, it has been to see
again, on every side, all the things I have
known. What! in eighteen centuries you
have accomplished only this! Nothing
new? Nothing better, truly? What I have

seen in your streets, in your parks, in your houses: is that all, is that really all? . . . How miserable, my friend!"

The astonishment she caused, held me speechless. She smiled and explained her-self:

"Thou seest how I am dressed?" she asked. "I am wearing the robe which was placed with me in the tomb. Behold it. In my time, one dressed in wool, in flax, and in silk. On returning to the earth, I thought to find these old stuffs lost even to memory. I imagined (forgive me) that after so many years men would have dis-covered marvelous tissues like the sunlight or moonlight and more delightful to touch than the skin of a virgin or of a fruit. But no; how do you clothe yourselves? in wool, in flax and in silk . . . Oh! I know:

you have found cotton, fit to clothe ne-
groes who were inconvenient in the state
in which they showed themselves. This
was, perhaps, extremely moral . . . Thou
likest cotton? Thou art proud of its discovery? As for me, I could not even feel
under my fingers this stuff which clings
and falls apart. Have you, indeed, a stuff
for covering better than wool? No. Finer
than the woven flax? more luminous than
silk? . . . But answer thyself."

She continued:

"In my day, we shod ourselves with
skins . . . We had sandals, colored shoes,
furred slippers, high boots . . . See: thine
own bicycling shoes, fastened with a loop
a little higher, are of Phrygian form. Look
at mine: they are of olive morocco, gilded
from little irons, like the binding of a book.

Admire them. Thou wilt find none so lovely in the shops of thy friends' trades men."

She continued further:

"In my time, to make jewelry, two precious metals were used: gold and silver. Have you found a third? Necklaces were made, rings, bracelets, ear-rings, diadems and brooches. I have found all these, identically, along the streets of Paris. You know the pearl, the emerald, the diamond, the opal, the moonstone, the ruby, the sapphire and all the tinted silicas which come from Arabia and India, today, as formerly. Have you, by any chance, created one precious stone in eighteen centuries? But one, tell me of one, I pray thee! one stone which I have not known, one ring which I have not had on my finger, one new

205

jewel, even mounted in gold like mine, since thou hast no rarer metal to offer me, but bearing in its claws a new gem?"

Her voice had become animated, little by little, to a tone of reproach and vexation. I made a quieting gesture.

"Callisto," I replied, "I think thou givest an exaggerated importance to the ornaments which women wear and which have no other purpose than to occupy, by their difficult choice and fastidious form, a stagnant and idle life. It is evident today, after ten thousand years of fruitless efforts among all people, that a young girl will never know how to be more beautiful by the art of the dress-maker, the embroiderer and the goldsmith than at the instant when she shows herself all naked, as the gods created her. I doubt not that the

Greeks knew this simple costume . . ."

"Better than thy compatriots."

"You did not invent it; do not be proud. I know that, in our days, it is travestied more painfully than in the time when thou wert born; but at the worst, of what importance is the difference. One cannot dress women. That is axiomatic. We cannot counteract it. If aesthetic truths could be demonstrated from theorems, M. Poincaire could already have proved mathematically that it is futile to exercise human imagination in an attempt to solve this problem; as certain an impossibility as the trisection of angles. For my part, I am not afflicted by a failure, which persists because it is eternal, and I am contented to admire woman in her primitive purity (which, for her, never changes) with the

207

antique emotion of those who once touched Helen."

She regarded me steadily and, inclining her head toward me, said slowly:

"Art thou sure, presumptuous one, that women have not changed?"

II

IN my agitation, I know not whether I saw what she did immediately after saying these words.

How she removed her rings, slipped off four bracelets, opened her necklace, let her vestments fall and, at the same time, her heavy hair, I could not say. It was so rapid and dazzling that it remains in my memory like a dim wonder.

Until then, I had not entirely believed in the reality of the adventure. Apparitions long believed supernatural and therefore recognized as obedient to the laws of a profound but unknown nature, some- times present themselves with the charac- ter of a material form which is not ques- tioned by any of our senses and which can mislead even a spirit which is incredulous or simply fortified against improbabilities.

For an hour, I had been asking myself whether I was not being mystified by some extravagant reader; some stranger, I thought, immodest enough and deliberate enough to come at night to a bed-chamber where she had certainly not been invited, wishing, no doubt, to cover the banal de- sign which moved her by a careful dissimu- lation under a costume from the theatre. I had responded in a mood to which she herself conducted me, with the reserve of a complaisant interlocutor who, through deference or curiosity, would not rend too quickly the tissue of a careful and interesting comedy.

But, as soon as she was nude, I knew that she had come to me from the distant past . . .

I remember very well that, at the moment I realized this, I approached, if I did not achieve, all the exaltation with which a religious instinct invincibly inspires me. I held myself in my chair to keep from falling on my knees and I gazed, my head forward, with a feeling of sacrilege, as though so marvelous a being should not be beheld by the same eyes which had seen mortal women. I had never known such agitation.

Callisto was superb. Her body was slender and rounded, the torso high, the legs

very long. Her fine joints were of a fragili-
ty which ravished me and even in the
muscular thighs one divined the delicate
bones. Depilated, but pure and without
cosmetics, her skin shone as though fresh
from the bath, browned in a light, uniform
tint, almost black about the breasts, along
the edges of the eye-lids and in the short
line of sex. I know not how to describe
her beauty which could never be devel-
oped in our climate or in our age, for it
was not born of any one detail but only
of harmony and perhaps of clarity. To
affirm a difference between her and the
women of my time, I was obliged to believe without any proof for my discern-
ment, as a collector distinguishes the true
from the false, sometimes without being

212

able to demonstrate the exact point upon which he establishes his conviction.

As though placing herself at my disposal, she extended herself upon a couch. "You could, at least, have perfected women," she resumed, smiling; "and, as thou seest, the races have deteriorated. Why have your doctors, who despise ours, left your mistresses, today, less beautiful than my sisters? The earth where we lived has not been engulfed. The Orontes descends always from the midst of the cedar mountains. Smyrna survives. Sparta is dead but Athens has been resurrected. Vain and feeble century, why hast thou replaced the Ionians with a mixture of Levantines and why hast thou not created selections of women as thou hast created

213

families of roses? Thou canst not. Thine effort is that of a child. Ours was that of gods."

While she spoke (I was scarcely in a mood to dispute with her), a terror such as one feels on the border of sleep pressed my temples. I trembled lest she leave me suddenly, like a fluid being born of the light; and I asked if my eyes only had the illusion of her corporeal present; if, with the tip of my finger, I could touch the delicate skin of her thigh.

"Come," she said, laughing, "I am not a shadow. Give me thy hand."

Arching her loins upon the couch, she passed my arm about her body which pressed voluptuously upon my fingers.

Then with a waywardness which

214

would take no denial, she resumed her discourse.

"A thousand years before the time of my beauty, men united with women somewhat as goats united. Thou hast read Homer? Neither Argos nor Troy knew of other pleasures than those contained in the savage acts of animals. Even the kiss upon the mouth was unknown to Briseis. Andromache never offered her breasts to other lips than those of her little child. About Helen's thighs no hand ever opened and lightly raised the shiverings born of the human caress."

She closed her eyes . . .

"And then, suddenly, in a day, the antique Orient where I was born took from the gods, like a fire eternally young, the

215

sole gift which distinguished them from the other inhabitants of the world: they discovered voluptuousness.

"O days of strength! Youth of the world! For the first time, the lips of a man and a woman, abandoning fruits, found themselves savory. The great burning soul of Aphrodite inspired the bodies of lovers and, each day, a new pleasure—a *new* pleasure, thou understandest—descended from blue Olympia into the great groaning beds. There was an unrestrained intoxication; from Babylon to Mount Erix, all the perfumes, all the silks, the flowers, the arts and the women, formed in the triumph which followed the discovery of pleasure. The young girls, at last liberated from hereditary barbarousness, conscious of their senses and of their desires, opened

216

their nostrils to the rose and their charming bodies to the mouth. During the centuries, the treasure of sensuality was aug-
mented. In my time, in Antioch and in
Alexandria, the women enriched it still
more. I myself, Callisto, the daughter of
Lamia, it is I who discovered this . . ."

But I drew back . . .

She laughed.

"Ah! Thou art afraid! Well then, speak
in thy turn; let us see! During the nine-
teen hundred years of my slumber in the
tomb, what unknown joy have you con-
quered? Not long ago I asked thee for a
new jewel. Now I ask thee for a love
which I have not already tried. Without
doubt, after so long a time, many new
pleasures have been discovered. I await
thine invitation to partake of them."

217

She was secure in her ironic position and I divined that, during her long nocturnal wandering about the city, she had tried in vain to augment her education; also, that I could offer nothing to this impossible search.

"Be patient," I said simply. "Thou seest, we have begun by forgetting everything. Later, we will re-invent. This is the history of modern civilization. It came to the world a few years after thy death, after unexampled calamities great enough to be irreparable. First came the birth and strange fortune of a religion which, in its origin, was certainly commendable but which, distorted by Israelites too rude or too adroit, rendered fruitless the efforts of thy race and scattered salt upon the ruins of Athens. Following this came the inva-

218

sions of Barbarians; when the deluge of Judea had rotted the wood of the vessel, the rats penetrated and scattered it in pieces. This endured until the new day when those books saved from destruction and recovered at Constantinople arose in the Orient like a new dawn. An hundred years were spent reading them. Since they have been studied, hardly three centuries have passed. But this age is for us, perhaps. We must be for the age, Callisto."

She smiled in derision.

"Have you found," she responded, "in the parchments of your museums, the tradition of Rhodopis? Can your archaeologists, who know so thoroughly the policies of Pericles and the strategy of Alexander, reconstruct the science of Aspasia and of Thais? Are they sure that the tomb in which the delicate ashes of Phryne repose, has not enclosed forever the secret of a lost voluptuousness?

"This tradition I have still. Wouldst thou know it? I will yield it to thee . . ."

III

WHATEVER may be the curiosity of the young girls who read this fragment of memories, I will not delay for a description of that which followed; first, because I have already written, upon the documents of Callisto, an entire book which is called "Aphrodite"; and in addition, because a certain reserve still restrains me, perhaps, from presenting, under a personal form, the details of a night of excesses.

Callisto arose toward noon. She caused me to observe pleasantly that the sun was already high and that, through need of a perfected lighting system, we had scarcely seen each other.

"You ruin the Night; you no longer know the Dawn," she said, sadly. "Formerly, the spectacle of the light of dawn was the recompense for long exhausting vigils. Now you pass your lives in a monotonous light and you no longer even know the Shadows."

I was uneasy.

"Noon! . . . But thou didst tell me of a life confined to nocturnal hours. How can I still hold thee here?"

"That is an affair between Persephone and myself," she replied, with a singular smile. "Let us talk. I have not finished abusing thine epoch."

I was a little tired and still nervous.

222

"Enough," I said, "I pray thee. Let us talk of ourselves, wilt thou? Let us leave the world, better or worse. . . I am interested only in thee."

"Still, hear me. Thou hast not been convinced. I will continue until thou art. Truly, I remain desolated at my second journey upon earth. I should have remained in the tomb, with the dreams of that purer age in which I grew up amidst pleasures. I need to tell someone about the deceptions which end my promenade and what I wish to thy century for all the surprises which it has not offered me. Thou seest, the world is a young man who gives hopes but who is likely to misfire his life."

"I know not. . . It seems to me that we have thought well and created well since thy death. The age in which we live is not so contemptuous."

"But it is! Partly from its impotence but more from its conceit. No; you have not thought and you have not created! You are Phoenicians, apt in reproducing the models invented by my race, but elsewhere than with us you find nothing, and you exist only in our shadow."

She made a gesture.

"Walk in the streets of Paris. Everywhere our eternal soul shines in the façades of the monuments, in the capitals of the columns and on the foreheads of the statues. After having built, during the barbarous and wretched middle-ages, those miserable buildings which are already (happily!) falling, you, the men of modern times, incapable of creation, have returned to our ruins and for four hundred years, have made mosaics of stone with the fragments of our temples. A column found in Sicily has engendered two thousand churches and as many railroad platforms. Even to new requirements you have not known how to give a new architecture. With the bronze of your cannons you have copied the Trajan column, and you have made concert halls in a Corinthian style. After us, with our sculptors who wrought in marble and cast in bronze, you have found nothing, not a natural stone, not a chemical alloy, worthy of reproducing the human figure. And the only glory of your sculptors is not from that which they have done, but because one has found, under the ground, a torso of Apollonius, a wreck without head, without arms and without legs, a lamentable ruin, but a created work, that; a creative work. Scholars!"

She took two books from a case and threw them upon the carpet.

"Your thought, like your art, is a parasite upon our cadavers. It is not Descartes, it was Parmenides who said that thought is identical with being. It is not Kant, it was still Parmenides who said that thought is identical with its object. In these two phrases, the modern schools are entirely encased; they cannot free themselves. Wherever our science became general, that is to say philosophical, there it has remained, to this day, upon our fundamental laws. The masters of Euclid fixed forever the unchangeable relation of lines. Archimedes supplied integral calculus long

before your Leibniz, who was equally in-
debted to us for his metaphysics. In place
of meditating upon the fall of apples, New-
ton, whom you venerate, could have lim-
ited himself to reading a page from Aristotle where his theory of universal gravity
was expounded two thousand years ago.
Upon the constitution of matter, which is
the problem of God, Democritus knew
more than Lord Kelvin; his hypothesis
alone remains admissible. Finally, at the
moment when you are upon the point of
conceiving a central and universal science,
with a law sufficient to explain all phe-
nomena—what is this science and what is
this law? No more than that to which
Heraclitus, two thousand four hundred
years ago, gave this definitive expression;
—fire transforms itself in movement;

movement transforms itself in fire; and that is the world."

I was exhausted.

"O Callisto," I supplicated, "hear my wingéd words; thou art much too learned. I had often heard that antique courtesans were women of rare intelligence, but it was not this, certainly, which made them so beautiful. Today, if Madame de Pougy, in spite of her great literary talent, wished to entertain M. Boutroux with the subjects which preoccupy him, she would not succeed in interesting him as much as an Aspasia speaking to Xenophon. And yet I would prefer to have her tell me more willingly about a robe from Jacques Doucet than about a thermo-dynamic law, and it is a conversation which would be more becoming to her supple body. Moreover, the charm of a woman always increases at the moment when she is silent; but this is a particular truth which is obvious only to men."

She waited silently until I had finished; then, with a victorious obstinacy, she resumed:

"How is it that, in two thousand years, you have discovered neither . . ."

"We discovered America," I interrupted, impatiently.

"That is not true!"

"Callisto, do not be absurd."

"I repeat, and I will maintain, that America was discovered by Aristotle and that this is not a paradoxical thesis but an historical and evident fact. Aristotle knew that the world is round and (as thou canst read in his books), he advised a search for

229

the road to the Indes 'by the west, beyond
the columns of Heracles. It was this proj-
ect which Columbus resumed. But one
has always reckoned that the glory of a
discovery remains with the brain which
conceives it and not with the one which
executes it. When Leverrier discovered
Neptune . . ."

"Ah, well," I said, consumed with lassi-
tude, "at least, thou wilt allow this: we
discovered Neptune."

"And when was that? Discovered Neptune! Thou art astonishing! Since yesterday I have been supplicating thee to reveal
a new pleasure to me, a conquest toward
happiness, a victory over tears. Neptune
has been discovered! I return to life, after
twenty centuries, concerned about every-

thing, jealous of the marvels I supposed invented, beseeching, if I were not to weep through my life of eternal shadow, to be returned quickly to the world; and someone has discovered Neptune! A pleasure! a pleasure! a pleasure of the spirit or a pleasure of the senses; it does not matter which! Must I descend again to the Elysian fields without bearing with me the quiver of a new pleasure?"

She extended her hands . . . Then, abruptly:

"Anyway, it was Pythagoras who discovered Neptune."

I subsided.

"Absolutely," she explained, inexorably, "Pythagoras found that the solar system was composed of ten stars. I do not know upon what he founded this number; but his disciple, Philolaos, came to discern, later, without any lensed instrument, and many centuries before Copernicus, the double movement of the earth upon its axis and about the central fire; although no doubt it is impossible for thee to really understand how such a discovery could have been established with the sole assistance of reason, thou hast no right to assume that the hypothesis of Pythagoras was advanced rashly and confirmed by accident. I have finished."

I contended no more.

"Wilt thou have a cigarette?" I asked.

"What?"

"I say: wilt thou have a cigarette? No doubt they also have come to us from

232

Greece. Perhaps it was Aristotle who ...."

"No. I had never seen them before. I admit that we were ignorant of this absurd habit which consists of filling the mouth with the smoke of leaves. But I do not suppose thou wouldst pretend to offer me this as a pleasure."

"Who knows. Hast thou tried?"

"Never! What, art thou also one of those who indulge in this ridiculous exercise?"

"Sixty times each day. It is, in fact, the sole regular occupation in which I willingly employ my life."

"And it pleases thee?"

"I really believe I could resign myself to not touching the hand of a woman for an entire week, sooner than separate from my cigarettes for the same length of time."

"Thou art exaggerating."

"Scarcely any."

She had become thoughtful.

"Ah well, give me a cigarette."

"I suggest it."

"Light it. What does one do? Breathe?"

"Young girls puff the smoke; but that is not the best way. It is better to really inhale. Draw in. Close the eyes. Again . . ."

After a few minutes, Callisto's little roll of oriental leaves was in ashes. She dropped the half-consumed end where the fard of her lips had left a trace of rouge.

There was a silence.

She would not look at me. She had taken the square package in her hand, which seemed agitated by a soft emotion, and, after she had examined it on all sides, I saw that she would not return it.

Slowly, with the care one bestows upon the most precious objects, she placed it near the ash-tray at the edge of a bright divan on which she stretched out her long, dark body.